STRIP TEASER

ROMEO ALEXANDER

ROMEO ALEXANDER

Published by Books Unite People LLC, 2021.
Copyright © 2021 by Books Unite People
All rights reserved.

No part of this book may be reproduced in any form or by any electronic means, including information storage and retrieval systems, without written permission from the author, except for the use of brief quotations in a book review.

This book is a work of fiction. All resemblance to persons living or dead is purely coincidental.

Editing by Jo Bird
Beta reading by Melissa R

DAN

If he'd known he was going to be in charge of the interviews, Dan wouldn't have suggested hiring more strippers.

Dan leaned forward onto the bar, looking at the man sitting next to him. "So, I'm not going to go through all the qualifications you put down. Truth be told, working a few months at a cafe really isn't going to help when it comes to taking your clothes off for a horny group of people drooling over you from a few feet away."

The interviewee, a young red head by the name of Aidan nodded, though Dan didn't miss how the man tried to cover up the small smile he almost let slip. They had only been sitting at the bar for about ten minutes while the rest of the employees at Nocturne began setting up for the night.

Dan had been working at the strip club for close to six years, and he still found it strange to see the place without the colorful lights cutting through the dark. The tables that lined the back wall of the first floor still had the chairs turned over on top of them, and the dance floor was dark and almost depressing looking. The overhead lights, bright and used only when the bar was closed, or they were chasing late-night stragglers out, cast deep shadows and always reminded Dan of the scenes in slasher movies where some poor bastard was inevitably about to be hacked and slashed.

"I'm not kidding," Dan told him, turning away from one of the two bars that sat at opposite ends of the first floor. He pointed past the main seating area and toward the center, where the raised dance floor sat. "You'd be performing there, and you see those short walls around the edges?"

"I do," Aidan assured him.

"Those are the only things that are going to be separating you from the people who came here to watch you shake your ass," Dan told him.

"Not just the walls," an absolute tank of a man told them in a low rumble as he passed, a large box in his arms.

"Yes, thank you, Glam," Dan told him with a scowl. "It's not like I was trying to make a point."

"Glam?" Aidan asked, peering over Dan's shoulder to watch the big man disappear through the back door.

Dan snorted. "That was my fault. First night he was working here, I got drunk off my ass and ended up putting this huge, sparkling tiara on him that came from a bachelorette party. I proclaimed him Glamorous and it just kind of...stuck."

"Is he...uh?" Aidan asked, still staring at the door.

"Into guys? Dunno, never asked and never seen him with anyone," Dan said, glancing back toward the stage. "But he's right, we always have security on hand in case someone gets a little too bold and tries to grab a dancer or get on the stage while they're performing. But it doesn't change the fact that, for the most part, you're kind of on your own up there. When the lights go down low, all those little panes of glass the stage is made of?"

"Yeah?"

"They light up, and you're center stage for the whole thing."

"No lights above?"

"No, there are. But we found that keeping the floor brighter during a show is a lot more fun for people than when it's mainly lit from above."

About once every six months, the manager and part-owner of the bar, Rico, called in a specialist company from a few hours south to come and check out the floor. Sometimes an individual pane had to be replaced due to damage, and sometimes the wiring had to be changed. Rico was insistent that the dance floor and stage were in working, safe shape. Dan couldn't exactly argue. The multicolored floor always looked brand new every time they turned it on.

Aidan glanced over his shoulder toward a flight of stairs that led to the second floor. "And what's that?"

"The VIP area," Dan told him, motioning toward the space that was, in fact, a closed-off room with wide windows looking down on the main floor. "People who are up there either paid for the privilege or they have connections."

"No private dance rooms?"

"Not for everyone. Only ones in Nocturne are up there in the VIP room and VIPs still have to pay for the privilege. And not one dancer here is obligated to do a private dance for anyone. If someone wants to work for just the dance floor tips, that's their choice."

Which honestly, was nothing to turn your nose up at. In the years he'd worked at Nocturne, Dan had rarely given a private dance to someone else, even if there was a demand for it at times. He had managed to live extremely comfortably off the money he made without ever needing to pad it with private dances. Of course, sometimes Dan had simply wanted to give one to a specific person, and other times the offer for giving one was just high enough that Dan didn't want to pass it up.

Some might call that greedy and shallow. Dan thought it was just business.

"So," Dan said, turning back toward the bar to look down at the man's application. "That's the basics of this place. There's a lot more to it, like getting used to doing different routines, helping out in cleaning up, and dealing with the crazy asses that work here."

"I think I can handle that," Aidan said with a small smile.

Dan eyed him for a moment, really taking him in. Aidan wasn't the biggest guy Dan had ever seen, but he wouldn't call the man short either. He had broad enough shoulders to stand out, but he wasn't built thick, and Dan guessed the man was more sleek than he was strong. There was definitely an innocent boy next door look to him, made all the more bright and shiny by his green eyes and the rarity of his shock of red hair.

He could definitely pull off the look, but it was the act that concerned Dan more.

Dan looked at the sheet again. "Well, I'll give you this much, you kind of hid something on your resume that you should have drawn more attention to."

"What's that?" Aidan asked, leaning over to look at the sheets with a frown.

"You listed being in the theatre back in high school," Dan said with a laugh, pointing at a line on one of the pages. "All things considered, that might work in your favor."

Aidan smiled at that. "Ah, yeah. Freshman year all the

way up until the end of my senior year. Got a couple of leads my junior year, but I got a part-time job in my senior one, so I tried not to go for important, time-consuming roles."

"Musicals?"

"Uh, sometimes. I'm not going to have to sing, am I?"

Dan chuckled, setting the pages down and leaning over the bar. "No, you're not going to have to sing. Well, unless that's something you'd want to do. Can't say we've ever had a singing stripper before, so that could draw some attention if you're good at it."

"I do alright," Aidan said with a shrug.

Dan was pretty sure that if Rico, the manager and the man who should have been doing the interview, was there, he would have probably denied Aidan. Rico was a good manager, and he seemed, in his own grumpy and standoffish way, to care about the people who worked under him. The thing was, he was incredibly picky and exacting, and he had no fear at turning people out the door if they didn't meet his entry requirements or if they repeatedly screwed up.

Aidan was just a little too quiet and came off as lacking confidence, two things that probably wouldn't make him a very good dancer. Yet, Dan's instincts told him that a knee-jerk dismissal of the other man might be a bad idea.

"Tell you what," Dan said, finally finding the bottle he was looking for and setting it on the bar. "I think I've heard and seen enough to say that you can go on to the next stage of this competition."

"Uh, competition?" Aidan asked, sounding worried.

Dan bent further over the bar, grunting as he tried to get the small fridge to open for him. "Yep. Interview, competition, whatever you want to call it. Personally, competition sounds like a lot more fun and high stakes, but you do you. Point is, can you come in...uh, next Wednesday?"

"What time?"

Dan grunted again, this time in pleasure as he got the door open. "Let's say six. We'll do the next interview as a group, and we can see whether or not you make the cut."

"A group? I didn't know there other people trying to get the job."

"Well, we can always use more dancers, even if they only sometimes show up," Dan said, rooting through the cooler. "But...well, you'll see when you get here. It's easier to explain once you're looking it in the face."

A deep chuckle stopped Dan's digging around. "Ah yes, the mysterious group interview. Got to have the cloak and daggers."

Dan grabbed the bottle of juice and sat back in his seat with a scowl. "Just when I think I have enough things to deal with tonight, trouble comes through the door."

Mateo shot him an easy grin as he leaned on one corner of the bar. "There's a certain degree of irony in you of all people calling someone else trouble."

Dan glanced at Aidan. "Ignore him. He's some drunk who wanders in here whenever he wants to cause trouble."

Mateo glanced at Aidan, winking. "I'm his best friend. And I used to work here."

Under his fake irritation, Dan was amused to see Aidan flush at the sudden attention from Mateo. Not that Dan wasn't used to that from people. Once upon a time, at the beginning of their friendship years ago, he had been just as prone to Mateo's easy charms. The man was built like a brick wall, and his dark, handsome features gave him an air of mystery and confidence that resulted in pure sex.

Dan hadn't exactly been able to behave himself, though

he wasn't alone in that. For the first year or two, both of them had carried on their friendship, though there were definite moments of sex thrown in there. It had been casual for them both, but when Dan slowly began to realize he was getting more than just friendly or sexual feelings for the other man, he had quickly backed off.

And he didn't regret it for a moment either. He much preferred having Mateo in his life as a friend than a lover. Plus, a few years back, Mateo had gone and found himself someone who had stolen his heart more cleanly than Dan had ever seen. Before Christopher, Dan would have believed that Mateo would end up single for the rest of his life, content to be by himself without a care in the world. And then one nerdy science professor from the local university had shown up at Nocturne one night and changed it all.

"Does your husband know you're here?" Dan asked with a raised brow.

"Fiancé," Mateo corrected, watching as Dan resumed making a drink. "And he doesn't require me to tell him where I'm at all the time. Plus, if I say I'm going to visit you, he knows that generally means coming here."

Dan pretended not to see Aidan deflate at the mention of Mateo's fiancé. "Alright, since he's here to give me shit, that means we're about done here. Just don't forget, Wednesday at six."

"Uh, yeah, sure, I can do that," Aidan said, sliding off the stool.

"Call ahead so we can get the door unlocked for you," Dan told him, his gaze sliding to Mateo. "Though apparently, we aren't keeping it locked during off-hours."

Mateo held up a ring of keys. "Rico never asked for it back."

Dan rolled his eyes, giving the metal shaker a vigorous

shake. "Of course, he gave you the chance to come in whenever you want. Between that and leaving me in charge whenever he goes on one of his impromptu vacations, I'm starting to think he's losing his mind in his old age."

Mateo plopped down on one of the stools. "He's like, what, forty-five? That's not old age."

"Early-onset Alzheimer's then," Dan said with a shrug as he poured the drink into a glass.

"I'm going to hazard a guess that isn't the case," Mateo told him with a smirk. "And since when do you drink at seven pm?"

"When I started having to come in at noon. I mean, for fuck's sake," Dan grumbled, motioning around. "I had to make sure the cleaning crew got here on time and did their shit right. Then I had to go through inventory and order everything that we needed, and I mean everything. Had to call that DJ and make sure he was still going to be coming in a few months or not because we never got a definitive answer."

Honestly, he was half-tempted to make a joke about the stress aging him, but even he had to admit that it wasn't the truth. While he wasn't getting quite the same attention he used to years ago, time had been kind to him. Thirty was just around the corner for him and while he'd lost some of the boyishness that had granted him his twinky look, he didn't think he looked bad.

Dan had known from pretty much his teens that he would always be smaller than most guys, that was just a fact of his life. And he was never going to fit into any shirts bigger than a small unless he wanted to swim in them. Thankfully, there were plenty of guys who very much enjoyed getting their hands on small dark-blond men. He also privately hoped the light brown eyes didn't hurt either, but Dan suspected most of them just liked the body he worked to keep in slim but toned shape.

"That DJ?" Mateo asked wryly. "Surely you can't mean my soon-to-be brother-in-law?"

"Yes, Devon," Dan said with a wave of his hand. "The giant goofball who is nothing at all like his brother. That one."

Dan vaguely remembered the man had played at Nocturne a few years before and to a very happy crowd as well. He remembered the man more than he remembered the music, and he wasn't sure if that was something the DJ would have liked to have heard. Fact was, the man was a taller, thicker, and infinitely more adorable version of his younger brother Christopher.

Not that Dan would ever lack the sense to tell Mateo or Christopher that.

"And then I had to sit through an hour and a half on the phone with Rico," Dan huffed, taking a drink. "I don't know why that man talks so damn much when he's on vacation."

"What did he want?" Mateo asked.

Dan sighed, setting the glass down with a thump. "Well, actually, I'm really glad you're here now that you've decided to bring it up."

Mateo snorted. "Man, that's a great way to start a conversation. Is this where I remind you that I'm not a stripper anymore?"

"Yes, yes, I know. You're no longer a filthy degenerate and don't strip for money. You just hold onto people while they tell you their problems and think about what you look like under those clothes," Dan said, waving a hand dismissively at him.

"First of all, yes, I don't strip for money. Secondly, I'm not a full therapist yet, you little brat," Mateo told him with a grin. "And lastly, and you can confirm this with Chris, I absolutely still am a filthy degenerate."

"I do vaguely recall what you were like behind closed doors," Dan said with an air of wistfulness.

Mateo grinned. "Before you get too distracted by going down memory lane, what do you need me for?"

"We've been having some...issues getting some new property," Dan said, meaning the club. "Apparently, the people in Scotsdale are hard-nosed sons of bitches, or the lawyers we keep trying to find are just wimps. I don't know, we've had two decide not to follow through with us in the past year and Rico is starting to lose his patience. And you know what he's like when he gets like that."

"Why is he buying more property?" Mateo asked. "I didn't know Nocturne was expanding."

Dan shrugged. "We've been making good money, and Scotsdale is just enough out of the way to not be big competition for Nocturne if we open up a place out there. But it's close enough that Rico could still drive there and not be on the road for hours if he has to. Nocturne has just been...steadily making money over the past few years, so Rico decided he wanted a new location."

When Dan had first learned about Nocturne after moving to the town of Greenford years before, he had been delighted and curious. It was the first time he'd ever heard of a co-ed strip club, just as happy to showcase female dancers as it was male ones. That it was also situated in the middle of a quiet little college town like Greenford had also intrigued him. Yet, it had never lost its popularity with the people of Greenford or the surrounding area, and profits had continued to roll in for everyone.

"Of course," Dan continued, rolling his eyes. "Scotsdale has some weird city statutes or something. So not only are we having to jump through hoops, but we can't actually set up a strip club there."

"Really?"

"I don't remember what they called it. Decency laws or something. Which is about as stupid sounding as it gets. Imagine having laws about decency. When you know damn well some of the fuckers that made that law probably come in here and drool over us when they think they can get away with it."

"Hypocrisy, thy name is politics."

"Right, so it's just going to be a club. Because getting drunk and stupid in public, while trying to get laid, is still somehow better than doing all that while someone waves their tits or crotch around on a stage."

Mateo chuckled. "Alright, I'm understanding the conundrum. But I'm not quite sure how I'm supposed to help you with that."

Dan grimaced and took another drink. "Your brother is a lawyer."

"You want me to ask Lucas if he'll help you?" Mateo asked with a raised brow.

"I mean, he's a lawyer. And one you know, so maybe he'll be a little more reliable?"

"You are aware that there are different types of lawyers, right?"

"This is me hoping he's the right kind of lawyer."

Mateo shook his head. "Well, if I remember right, he did a bit of dabbling back in the day with property law. I have absolutely no idea if he'd be willing."

"Can you ask?" Dan asked. "I told Rico I would figure something out before he got back and if I don't, I'd like to at least show that I gave it a shot."

Mateo shrugged. "I can ask him next time I see him.

We're doing our family dinner on Sunday anyway, so that'll be a good time to nail him down for some questions."

If Dan had to wait a few days for an answer, he would happily make himself be patient. Rico was pushing to get moving on finding a place and buying it, not to keep pushing back the timetable. And if Dan made the man's life easier, then he would be making his own life easier as well.

"Awesome," Dan said with a notable amount of relief. "If he says yes, just give him my number and we can set up a time to meet and talk things through. He'll still need Rico, but at the very least, I can give him an idea of what he has to look forward to."

Mateo hummed thoughtfully. "Yeah, about that. Don't hit on him."

"What?" Dan asked, blinking.

Mateo smirked. "I know your type. He's straight, so don't try."

"You know I love a challenge."

"If you want to scare away another lawyer because you got horny, that's on you. I'm not going to save you if you hump his leg."

"That's so rude."

"Yet accurate."

"It was one time and the guy asked for it, and in a private dance, you fucker! You promised not to speak a word to anyone about it," Dan told him with a scowl.

Mateo grinned. "And I haven't. I'm talking to you about the time you dry-humped a guy's leg to get him off."

Dan froze when he heard Glam's voice behind him. "He did what?"

"Oh," Mateo said, hissing between his teeth. "Damn, Glam, when did you get there?"

"Like a dog?" Glam asked in bewilderment.

Dan groaned, thumping his head on the bar. "I hate you."

"No, you don't," Mateo told him, taking his drink and downing the rest of it. "You love me."

"With a friend like you, who needs an enemy?" Dan grumbled, yanking the glass out of his hand. "I said you were coming in here to cause trouble."

Mateo gave him an innocent look. "I don't know what you mean."

But he did, they both did, and Dan could hear the others calling out curiously from the back at Glam's shocked tone. Now everyone was going to find out about that particularly odd incident and Mateo was just going to sit there and grin about it.

He needed new friends.

LUCAS

Lucas frowned as he listened to the man on the other end of the phone. He was beginning to wonder why he'd chosen to come in on a Sunday. Admittedly, his bosses had been pushing that they might be looking for someone to play a third partner at the law firm and that not so subtle hint had grabbed Lucas's attention. If he could prove himself to be a little more dependable and a go-getter, it might put him higher on the list.

"No," he told his client, doing his best to keep the annoyance from his voice. "I don't think you should be talking to her anymore. Richard, listen to me, you're currently being charged with harassment and assault. The last thing you should be doing is trying to 'clear things up' with her. That's just going to get you arrested again."

"It's bullshit," the man vented in his ear. "She's getting on Facebook and Twitter, telling everyone about this shit, and I didn't do anything! I can't even go to work without people thinking I've been stalking her. All I wanted was for her to leave me alone and now I'm looking to go to jail."

"You're not going to go to jail," Lucas assured him. "At

worst, you'll have to pay a fine or do some community service."

"I shouldn't have to!"

Lucas sighed, thinking that the number of times he'd heard that phrase from a client ranked right up there with 'it isn't fair'. The sad fact of life was the justice system wasn't as much about justice as it should have been or was touted to be either. More often than not, lawyers weren't battling it out to show the truth, they were finding ways to bend the truth and the rules enough to make their side come out as the winner.

Lucas often thought it was no coincidence that many lawyers ended up as politicians.

"That's the worst-case scenario," Lucas promised him, turning to eye his computer to see how much longer until he could leave. "At best, we show that you have been keeping your distance for months leading up to the incident. And, that you didn't start the fight, but her brother did."

"Well, he did," Richard grumbled in his ear, though Lucas noted the man had calmed down.

"I know," Lucas told him.

He honestly thought it was a lot more messy than that, but he knew better than to show even the slightest doubt to a client. The only thing worse would be to show doubt to the opposing legal team. Muddying the waters was one of the most sure-fire ways in which to make a case crash and burn, and generally speaking, whoever wasn't responsible for muddying the water was the one caught on the back foot.

Did he believe that Richard hadn't been harassing his ex-girlfriend and that, in fact, it had been his ex who had been stalking Richard? Yes, he did. There was enough evidence littered about the place that Lucas was still collecting to prove that. Did he believe that Richard was truly guiltless on the night he drove to her house to confront her after weeks of trying to get her to back off from a safe distance? Not entirely, no. There had been enough alcohol in the man's system to make him stupid, and while he was pretty sure the ex-girlfriend's brother had thrown the first punch, he was quite sure it hadn't gone unprompted.

But those were thoughts he kept to himself, especially now he had the client calmed down.

"I know this process is draining and frustrating," Lucas told him. "I've seen it happen more than once. But the worst thing you can do right now is give them the ammunition they need to make your life miserable. As your lawyer, I would strongly advise you to say nothing, do nothing, not one thing that could be used against you. Don't contact them, don't argue with them or their friends and family online. Just take screenshots of everything and send them on to me."

"Will that help?" Richard asked hopefully.

"It might," Lucas told him, though he doubted it. Most juries didn't care if people were already assumed guilty by the public. "But even if it doesn't, you can certainly use everything you'll collect to sue them for damages if we get you off."

Ironically, he had come to find that civil court cases tended to work out for falsely accused parties. Sure, the criminal courts might acquit someone, but that didn't do a damn thing to repair the damage done to their lives and reputations. Lucas had watched people's entire lives fall apart despite being found not guilty by a jury of their peers. It was the biggest reason he always told his clients to keep evidence of everything someone accusing them of a crime did.

"Well, I can do that," Richard told him, now sounding a little put out. "I don't know what I'm going to do if I lose my job, though, man. Like, it's all I got now."

"I understand," Lucas told him earnestly. "I've been on the receiving end of a few vengeful exes myself."

"Yeah, love's a bitch ain't it?"

"It can be. But that doesn't mean you have to be its bitch. Just let me do my job, keep your nose clean, and keep a record of everything. Okay?"

It took a little longer for him to get Richard off the phone finally, but he hung up hoping he'd got through to the man. Some days, Lucas didn't know what was the most difficult part of his job, the occasional long stretches of monotonous paperwork, the opposing legal teams, or the clients themselves.

At the very least, the end of the call signaled the end of his day. Since it was the weekend, he only had to come in for half a normal day, and he was almost an hour past that. He would have enough time to get home, change, and then drive out to his mother's for the family dinner they'd held every Sunday for years.

And that thought was enough to bring a slight bounce to his step as he closed down the office for the day.

HE HAD JUST MANAGED to switch off the engine when a familiar scarf-covered head rounded the back of his car. Lucas sighed as he heard the crunch of gravel, knowing full well his mother had waited for him to drive up and was about to ambush him.

"Hi, Mom," he said as he pushed the driver's side door open to let the summer sunlight stream onto his face.

"Hello, Lucas," she said pleasantly, squinting down at him. "Nice of you to show up after the worst of the cooking is over."

"Because I planned it that way," Lucas told her, waiting until she stepped back to get out of his car.

"Considering how bumbling you are in the kitchen, I might believe it," she told him, peering up at him.

"I was working," he said, trying to defend himself against a woman who came up to his chest.

"I'm well aware," she told him, shaking her head. "It's Sunday. It's the day of rest."

"Are you getting religious on me, Mom?"

"It doesn't take religion to appreciate an excuse to relax."

Lucas chuckled, bending down to hug her. "I think I'll let you and Mat do all the relaxing. I've still got plenty of things I have to do through the week."

She hugged him back with surprising vigor. "That's what you always say. And you need to learn to slow down, I've always told you that."

Ever since his growth spurt at the age of fourteen, Lucas had gotten used to having to bend down to hug her and practically put his chin to his chest to look her in the eyes when she stood before him. Mateo had been the same way a couple of years later when puberty kicked in full force for him. It didn't change the fact that Emelia knew exactly how to keep her boys in line because neither of them would have ever had the heart to disrespect or upset their mother.

"Yes, you do tell me every time I see you on Sunday," Lucas said in agreement, letting her out of his arms. "And I tell you every time that it isn't going to happen. Perhaps we could find a nice middle ground, a way to have the conversation shorthand without having to go through the whole song and dance."

"Not likely," she told him with a swat. "Now get in there and get yourself cleaned up. Christopher is about to put the food out."

"Yes, Mom," he told her fondly, turning to walk up the brick-laid steps surrounded on each side by plants and across the large front porch into the hallway.

The smell of food, rich and savory, filled the space as he took a detour into the hallway bathroom. Whatever his soon-to-be brother-in-law had cooked smelled like it was heavy on the meat and not so light on the spices. When Christopher had first started dating Mateo, the man had suffered through trying to adjust to the amount of heat their family put into their food. It had taken a little while, but Lucas could confidently say the man could keep up with the rest of them when it came to spicy food.

When Lucas was done, he stepped out of the bathroom and into the kitchen. He managed to step inside before stopping dead in his tracks. Rather than finding Christopher merrily finishing up the last of the meal, Lucas instead found the man pressed against the fridge and Mateo's tongue down his throat. And, much to his horror, he was fairly sure that one of Mateo's hands had found its way into Christopher's pants.

"Really?" Lucas asked loudly.

Mateo grunted in surprise, pulling back, and there was just enough of a gap between the two men for Lucas to see that a hand had indeed been down the front of Christopher's pants. The smaller man was flushed, but Lucas didn't think it had anything to do with being busted. No, Christopher had been dating Mateo for too long, and the quiet, incredibly well-behaved and mild-mannered Christopher had become far more laidback and willing to misbehave.

"Please tell me you're going to wash your hands," Lucas said, plopping down at the table in the middle of the kitchen and staring down rather than at his brother and his fiancé.

"Yes," Christopher told him, having the decency to sound embarrassed.

"Don't you guys get enough of that at home?" Lucas asked, shuffling his silverware around on his napkin. "I mean, you live together, for fuck's sake."

"Language," his mother chided as she entered the room behind him.

"Well then, scold the two getting handsy in your kitchen," Lucas complained, jabbing an accusing finger at Mateo who he knew damn well was the truly guilty party.

Their mother looked at Mateo, narrowing her eyes. "Did you get all the rocks where I told you to put them?"

"I was going to finish up after dinner," Mateo told her. "I knew dinner was just about done."

"I had better not go out there and find that you lazed around until dinner," she told him, inching toward the door. "Especially when I find out that you're trying to screw poor Christopher over the counter."

"Oh god, it wasn't that bad," Lucas protested with a groan.

"It was against the fridge," Mateo told her, following her out the door and complaining loudly. "And the counters aren't high enough for me to make it work right for us here!"

"Why are they like this?" Lucas asked, shaking his head.

Christopher glanced over at him, smiling softly. "Because they're a lot alike. Well, and I think they like embarrassing us too."

"You don't seem very embarrassed," Lucas pointed out.

Christopher cleared his throat, turning back to the stove to start pulling things off the burners. "Yes, well, I suppose Mateo has been a big influence in that regard. It's difficult to be too bashful and easily embarrassed when you've chosen to spend the rest of your life with a man who doesn't know the meaning of shame."

"I think I'm the only one who got that gene," Lucas muttered.

Christopher chuckled as he brought the large pot of chili over and dropped it onto the hot pad at the center of the table. "Well, I hope for the sake of the women you date that you take after him in *some* ways."

Lucas groaned. "God, remember when you could barely bring yourself to say anything at the dinner table unless directly asked?"

Christopher continued to chuckle as he gathered up the seasonings to place on the table as well. "That is, if you're ever planning on dating again. If not, I'm sure we can find you a monastery you can spend the rest of your life at. Surely they're in need of a lawyer."

"And now I have to say you've been spending too much time around my mother," Lucas complained. "Seriously, why do I come to these dinners?"

It wasn't like there wasn't some truth to the accusation. Lucas honestly could not remember the last time he'd gone on a date, let alone tried to have a relationship. His last relationship had been almost three years before, and he was pretty sure there was an angry realty agent by the name of Kimberly who still bore him a longstanding grudge.

Just as the words left his mouth, Mateo came stomping into the house, rolling his eyes. "I don't know why you're complaining, it's not like you're not going to use Lucas and me to do the rest of the job anyway."

"Not the point," their mother told him, following her youngest with a raised brow. "If you weren't so focused on trying to get your kinky rocks off in my kitchen, you might have got a little more done."

"That's why," Christopher told him with a smirk.

"You and I have very different ideas of what good motivation is," Lucas said dryly.

Mateo rolled his eyes and plopped down in the seat across from Lucas. "Please tell me you guys are talking about something interesting. Please."

"I was wondering if Lucas got any of the same genes you did when it came to the bedroom," Christopher told him.

"Oh, that's an interesting question," their mother said as she slid into her own seat.

"No, it's not," Lucas told them. "New subject."

"Then we can talk about the fact that you've been single for way too long?" Christopher suggested.

"No, not that either."

"That you haven't had a proper vacation in almost two years?"

"Try again."

"Fine," Christopher sighed, though Lucas could see the man was still enjoying himself. "Then I seem to have run out of things to bring up."

Lucas almost asked the man how his mother was doing but bit his tongue at the last second. It had been a few years since the relationship between mother and son had deteriorated. Lucas still didn't know all the facts, but he knew enough to know that Christopher's mother had been a difficult woman who had made it her sole duty to dictate every little thing that happened in Christopher's life, even while the man was an adult. It had come to a head when Christopher had been dating Mateo early on, and his relationship with his mother hadn't truly recovered.

In fact, Lucas suspected it never truly would, which was precisely why he needed to keep his mouth shut.

Mateo began spooning food into Christopher and then his mother's bowl. "Well, it just so happens that I have something to talk to you about."

Lucas held out his bowl for his brother to fill, wrinkling his nose. "I don't think I want you to bring up a subject. Really, I would be happy if everyone just didn't talk because it seems like today is 'poke your nose in Lucas's business day'. And really? Not a fan."

Mateo smirked, finally filling up his own bowl. "Lucky for you, I'm not here to talk about your personal life. Even if it could use a little sprucing up."

"You all act like I'm becoming some spinster, whittling away at the remainder of my life instead of going out to find true love," Lucas grumbled.

They meant well, they really did, but he didn't need them worrying after him because of his love life of all things. There were some good points about taking time off, sure, but his love life? No, he was perfectly fine with the way things were and not in any rush to change things.

"No, it's actually about business, if you can believe it," Mateo said with a chuckle. "A little favor for me, if you're willing."

"You know it would be a conflict of interest for me to represent you," Lucas told him with a frown. "And why would you need my help? Since when did you get in trouble?"

"Streaking through the town center," Mateo told him with a shrug.

Christopher rolled his eyes. "He did not."

"I would believe it," Lucas said.

"So would I," their mother added.

Mateo snorted. "No, turns out Nocturne is trying to get some property up in Scotsdale to open up a new club. The non-stripping kind. And I guess they've been having trouble keeping a lawyer. Dan pretty much begged me to see if you might be willing to help."

"Property law isn't exactly my expertise," Lucas said slowly.

"No," Mateo agreed. "But I remember that the first office you worked at, they threw you a lot of property cases."

"Yeah, because they had enough criminal defense lawyers as it was," Lucas said with a frown. "It's why I inevitably left, to practice what I'd studied for. But that was...quite a while ago, Mateo."

Their mother chuckled. "You've always had a steel trap for a brain. There's no way you didn't retain a lot of what you read and had to go through."

"Maybe," Lucas said slowly, smiling a little at the praise. "But that wouldn't make me an expert."

"Well, I don't think they need an expert," Mateo told him. "Just someone to go through the process instead of bailing out on them. They already know what they're supposed to build and not supposed to build, so I don't think they need someone who's an absolute expert in the field."

"Well," Lucas said, pushing the remainder of his chili around the bottom of the bowl. "I suppose it wouldn't hurt to at least meet and find out what needs to be done. If I can't manage it, or I think it needs someone a little more specialized, I can always recommend someone far more reliable."

Mateo brightened. "So, you'll do it?"

Lucas shrugged. "I don't see why I couldn't give it a try. Might be a nice break from what I've been doing lately."

"And you'll finally get to see Nocturne," Mateo said with a grin.

Lucas narrowed his eyes. "Please tell me this was not some convoluted attempt to get me to go into that strip club."

Mateo laughed. "No, it's just a nice bonus, is all."

"He has his priorities straight," Christopher said with no small amount of fondness.

"Eh," Mateo shrugged. "Dan seemed like he could really use the help, so I figured I might as well ask. Thank you, though, I mean it."

Lucas waved him off. "Don't thank me until I've actually done something."

Mateo smirked, glancing at Christopher. "You'd think that was a sign that he's humble, but he's really not."

"Oh no," their mother said, eyeing Lucas fondly. "Not a humble bone in that one. He'll make sure to get the job done before he starts strutting about. And not a moment sooner."

"You'd think that was praise," Lucas told Christopher. "But in fact, it's them giving me shit because they think that counts as love and affection."

"It does," both his mother and brother announced.

Lucas sighed, shaking his head. "Oh, my family."

"You love us," they said in unison again.

DAN

"Hey, Dan?"

He pulled his head up from the paperwork he was going over. While Rico was away on his vacation, Dan had taken over the man's workspace. It wasn't the first time he'd done it, but Rico always bitched that Dan 'messed up' everything whenever Dan was left in charge. Which was, in Dan's opinion, a blatantly incorrect statement. All he did was tame the absolute rabid mess that was Rico's office whenever he was supposed to be in it.

Dan looked at Glam, who was waiting patiently in the office's doorway. "What's up?"

"There's some suit at the front door," Glam told him. "Says he's here to talk to you? I made him wait to make sure it wasn't another stalker."

Dan inwardly cringed at the reminder of why they had two vacant spots in their dancer lineup. He couldn't blame TJ for having left, the poor guy had been dealing with a stalker following him everywhere and had started taking refuge in Nocturne, where the stalker was barred from entry. That had all come crashing down when it had only been he and a couple of other people, including a long-time dancer at Nocturne, Rhonda.

The woman had sworn up and down that she didn't know a thing about TJ's stalker trying to constantly get to him. And that she had only let the man into the club because he'd been 'really nice and polite' and had said he had an appointment to inspect the wiring. This, despite everyone being told to keep a look out for the guy, and that no one was ever to be allowed in during non-business hours unless Rico personally let them in.

It had been ugly. TJ had been cornered and the stalker apparently wasn't shy about using his fists. He'd beaten the hell out of the poor guy in the backroom before Glam could hurry his way back there. TJ had quit, which honestly Dan didn't blame him, and was privately thankful they hadn't ended up being sued. Rhonda had been fired, and while Dan had felt a small twinge of pity for the woman, it hadn't been enough for him to argue against Rico's decision.

"If it's Mateo's brother, just bring him back here," Dan told him.

Glam nodded and disappeared back into the hallway. He knew full well that the man would personally escort Lucas to the office and linger to make sure everything was okay. The incident with TJ had bothered Glam more than anyone. Dan suspected it was because Glam had been security that day and hadn't even known that there was danger in the building while he was up checking the VIP rooms. The man took his job very seriously, and that night had been the only time Dan had ever seen Glam lose his temper.

Glam reappeared a couple of minutes later with someone at his side. The man was only a little shorter than Glam, which was impressive by itself. He wasn't built the same, though his shoulders were nearly as broad, his waist was tapered and accentuated by the tailored suit he wore.

"Lucas, I take it?" Dan asked as he stood up.

"Yes," Lucas told him, holding his hand out. "And you would be Dan?"

Dan took the man's hand, feeling his strong grip and shaking it firmly. It was a little difficult to see how the man could be related to Mateo in the slightest. Mateo was built a little bit more like Glam but shorter than both men standing before Dan. He was also dark, whereas Lucas was a very light blond, and instead of dark brown, his eyes were grassy green.

And he was already proving far too well behaved to be related to Mateo.

"I'm surprised Mateo didn't give you my stage name instead," Dan told him, motioning to one of the seats in front of the desk. "Have a seat if you want."

Lucas snorted softly. "I'm sure if he'd been thinking, he would have tried. Thankfully, he decided to make things simple."

"That doesn't sound like the Mateo I know."

"He has his moments. Few and far between, but they're there."

It was said with a faint smirk and Dan saw what he'd been missing before. Dan supposed it made sense that the family resemblance would show itself in an expression Dan had witnessed on Mateo's face quite often. It was supposed to be an expression of amusement, but on Lucas's face, just as it always was on Mateo's face, there was a smugness there that amused Dan.

"Well," Lucas began, pulling a decent sized tablet from the bag he brought with him and turning his attention to it.

"Admittedly, Mateo didn't tell me very much about the situation, just a very brief overview."

"To be fair, I didn't offer up too much information," Dan admitted. "And after he told me you weren't exactly a property specialist, I wasn't all that hopeful that you'd take an interest."

Lucas hummed thoughtfully, nodding his head. "I'm not. But he knew to ask me because I spent far longer than I should have at the last law office I worked, having property issues being thrown onto my desk. So I gained my fair share of experience. That being said, if I'm unable to help you properly, I know a few people I can make a call to who won't bail on you, especially if I ask it of them."

It was interesting, listening to Lucas talk. The man was clearly far more formal and careful in his speech, whereas Mateo had been laid back and confident from the very start. Not that Lucas didn't come across as self-assured, he obviously knew what he was talking about and believed in it. But there was a great deal more professionalism in him, though that might have had more to do with the setting than anything else. Dan wondered if the man would be the same if the setting was more casual and quietly regretted never asking Mateo about his older brother.

"I would appreciate that," Dan told him, setting the paperwork before him into a pile off to the side. "Truth be told, I've been a little desperate to get some help with this. I'm sure Mateo told you, but the last two we brought on board decided to leave before we could close on anything. The first was because of health issues, but the second said something about 'personal differences' preventing them from continuing."

"Interesting," Lucas said, looking up from the device. "Did you happen to keep the contact information for the last one? I'd be interested to see what he has to say. That is if he's willing to talk in the first place."

"I'm sure I have it here somewhere," Dan said, looking around the desktop and rooting through the drawers with a frown. "Honestly, I hate how much of a disaster it is in here. I've barely had a chance to do a thing with it."

"A little organization can help," Lucas said, though his attention was back on the tablet, and Dan had no idea what he was doing.

Dan huffed. "I've told Rico a thousand times that he could get more done if he didn't stack everything wherever he felt like it. Then he goes and leaves me in charge and expects me to somehow know where anything is in this absolute disaster."

Lucas looked up, cocking his head. "Interesting. I thought you were the one in charge."

Dan snorted, turning around to open the drawers in the cabinet behind him. "At the moment, yes. But that's not really my main job around here. I just take over whenever Rico decides he's had enough nudity for a time and goes somewhere else."

"And where is he right now?"

"In Vegas, looking at strippers."

"I..."

Dan fished the cards out of a bottom drawer and grinned at Lucas's nonplussed expression. "I never said it had to make sense."

"So I see," Lucas said with a faint snort. "Well, I'm afraid there isn't much I can do unless I'm talking with the person whose name will be on the sale."

"That'll be Rico and the other owner, Jacob Masters," Dan told him, holding out the cards from the last two lawyers. "At the moment, I'm just trying to get someone in here who'll be able to help us if they can. If you're game for that, I'm more than happy to connect you with Rico and give you Jacob's number if you want."

"Does the other owner, Mr. Masters, come around here often?" Lucas asked, tapping away now.

Dan shook his head. "Not really his kind of place. He only invested because he saw the money this place could make. For the most part, he's pretty happy to let Rico do his thing and call it good, especially considering how well it's done. But Jacob just so happens to be dating my best friend, so I have ready access to him if I need it."

"Well, that's convenient," Lucas said with a faint chuckle.

"Yeah, my friend used to be an escort, which is how Jacob met him."

"O-oh?"

Dan chuckled. "Yeah. Jacob was looking for a piece of arm candy to show off and pretend like he had a boyfriend so other people would stop trying to get in his business and hook other people up with him. And that's how he met Max, so they could fake date for a couple of months. Well, joke was on them, they fell for each other and the sentimental bastards still celebrate their anniversary on the day they agreed to make their little contract rather than when their real relationship started."

Personally, Dan was pretty fond of the story because he thought it was about as unusual as it got. From the curious expression of thought on Lucas's face, Dan figured he wasn't the only one. Most people, when they heard the story, were too dumbfounded to speak at first and then tried to figure out how they were meant to react.

"Well," Lucas said with a cock of his head. "I can't say

I've ever heard that one before. But I can't say much, especially if it works for them."

"Oh, it does," Dan assured him, leaning back in his seat. "The bastard's had better luck with love than I've ever come close to, and they did it by accident."

Lucas snorted, nodding his head. "I'm quite familiar with the feeling."

"Really?" Dan asked in genuine surprise. "You don't strike me as someone who would have too much trouble."

Lucas blinked. "And why is that?"

"Well," Dan motioned to Lucas, and more toward the way his tailored suit didn't do much to hide the obviously well-cared-for body. And then up to his face, which, while it didn't resemble Mateo's directly, obviously came from a good gene pool. "Quite frankly, you're pretty hot, dude."

Lucas blinked again. "Thank you. Though as I've found out, that doesn't exactly help me when it comes to luck in love."

"I'm sure it helps getting people into bed."

"It would, if I were the sort."

"Ooh, well behaved."

"In theory."

Dan grinned in delight at that. "Oh, so you're just a one girl for a long time kind of guy. But that doesn't mean you're clean and innocent."

Lucas continued to stare at him without changing his expression. "I've yet to have any complaints. At least about anything done in private, that is."

"That's a shame," Dan said with a wistful sigh.

"And why's that?"

"Because you're good-looking, apparently fun when you're alone with someone but terminally straight."

"Terminally," Lucas repeated, deadpan. "That's certainly one way to put it."

Dan laughed. "I promised Mateo I would behave myself and now I'm seeing why he told me in the first place. Well, other than the fact that I'm a flirt."

"I hadn't noticed," Lucas said, with the slightest hint of a curl at the corner of his mouth.

Dan grinned. "I can't help it. Get me around a good-looking guy, and suddenly I start talking to the good-looking guy and telling him he's good-looking. It's a whole cycle that just repeats itself and I can't make it stop sometimes."

"One might call it terminal," Lucas said with a wry raise of his brow.

"Careful," Dan warned him. "Keep talking like that and I'll think you have a sense of humor."

"And if I do?"

"Then I'm going to have to call your terminal case of heterosexuality a tragedy."

That earned him a real smile. Dan wasn't surprised in the slightest to find that again, there were similarities between the brothers. Yet there was a difference, although Mateo could be warm and affectionate, very easily, in fact, even his genuine smiles radiated an obvious aura of confidence. While Lucas's smile mirrored his brother's in appearance, the feel of it didn't quite have that background emotion of confidence. Instead was just a truly nice smile that Dan could appreciate.

"I can see why my brother gets along so well with you. There's a lot of similarities between you."

"Ooh," Dan grunted. "I'm not so sure that's a good thing. Especially since Mateo has been pretty honest about how much he drives you crazy whenever he sees you."

"That's brothers for you," Lucas said with a light shrug.

"I know he doesn't mean anything by what he says, and he knows I'm not genuinely taking offense. I do know that it entertains him to irritate me, and I don't mind giving him the reaction he's looking for."

"Aw, that's sweet," Dan told him with a wink. "Brotherly love."

"Any siblings of your own?" Lucas asked.

Dan shook his head. "Just me and my dad. My mom didn't even wait until I was one year old before taking off to who the hell knows where. So he took care of me."

"Oh, he never remarried?"

"Ah, well, actually he did, pretty recently," Dan said with a chuckle. "I officially have a step-dad now."

"Oh," Lucas said, eyes widening slightly.

Dan laughed. "Yeah, turns out my dad was a little on the fence about who he was into. He met Keith when I was...uh...eleven or twelve, somewhere in there. Of course, at the time, my dad was trying to pass him off as a friend. But then I got a little bit older and figured out where my interests sat and I was the one who sat him down. Had to tell him I already knew about him and Keith and that it was fine, and it would make it a hell of a lot less awkward if I ever brought a boyfriend home."

Lucas set the tablet in his lap, raising a brow. "You were thirteen when you sat your father down, outing him, and then outing yourself?"

"Yeah," Dan said with a shrug. "My dad has always been the quiet type, really private. Don't know how the hell he managed to raise a big mouth, no shame punk like me, but he did. So yeah, if I didn't say anything, he was going to keep hiding it when there wasn't any reason. Hell, even if I had been into women, God forbid, I wouldn't have cared."

"God forbid," Lucas repeated, sounding faintly amused.

"What? Have you seen guys?"

"I'm familiar with men, yes."

"Yeah, well, you're not *familiar* familiar. And let me tell you, guys are hot. Not that women can't be or whatever, I know that's your thing, but c'mon, *men*."

"I can't say I've ever had a chance or reason to understand," Lucas told him and Dan would swear the man was trying not to laugh.

Dan snorted, waving a hand at him. "You have no idea how much you're missing. Ask Mateo."

"Ugh. My brother is a little too liberal with his personal life, especially now that he and his fiancé are around the house all the time," Lucas told him with a wrinkle of his nose.

Dan laughed again, nodding. "Yeah, the few times they've both come in here over the past year or so, I've noticed Chris is uh...well, he's still Chris, but he's loosened up a lot."

"I imagine it's good for him. After having to live under his mother's oppressive thumb for so long, a bit of freedom is bound to be healthy," Lucas said.

Dan nodded, knowing that much about Christopher's personal history. "I know it's made Mateo happy."

Again, there was that smile, with a little more warmth added in. "Yes. Christopher has made my brother incredibly happy, and I'm happy for both of them. I just wish they didn't feel the need to grope each other wherever they went."

"Don't even get me started," Dan said with a laugh. "I caught them getting a little too handsy in the VIP booth once. And worse, they didn't let me watch!"

Lucas shook his head. "And now I know why Mateo

never brought you around the house. Within an hour, our mother would have tried to adopt you."

"Really?" Dan asked with interest. "Well, now I'm sad that I've never got to meet her."

A knock interrupted them as Glam leaned in, wincing apologetically. "Hey, that one dancer you interviewed is here for his second round."

Dan grinned, looking at Lucas. "So, up for a little bit of a free show?"

"I'm afraid I'll have to give you a rain check on that...indefinitely," Lucas told him as he stood up. "Stripping has never really been my thing."

"Well, I'm not asking *you* to get up there," Dan told him, though privately he wouldn't have objected to the idea. "We like to bring our interviewees in for their second interview and have them do an impromptu dance for everyone who works here."

"Really?" Lucas asked as he tucked his tablet away. "And does that work?"

"Well, it's certainly worked so far," Dan told him. "They're never warned what's about to happen. They're told to come in, and when they do, we have them pick a song and, if they want, an outfit and then perform for us. Rico's logic has always been that if they can't perform for the few of us here without warning, then they're not going to make it when they have to dance for a bigger group of strangers."

"A little trial by fire," Lucas said, which earned a nod from Dan.

"It can seem a little mean, I guess, but it's worked out for all of us. Most of the people who get through the ordeal are generally ones who get to work the stage for real."

"Most?"

"Well, most of them aren't that good at first, but the willingness to do it is what counts. But some just...are really bad at dancing and there's not much that can be done about that."

"No amount of teaching helps?"

Dan snorted. "Trust me, some people? They just can't dance for the life of them. You should see my friend Max. Two left feet, no rhythm to save his life, and is more likely to step on your feet than on the ground."

"Shame," Lucas said, tucking his bag under his arm. "Dancing can be quite enjoyable if you have the right partner."

Which would have been the prime time for a comment about how sex worked the same way, and also the moment to ask if Lucas would be interested in showing Dan his moves on an upcoming night, say at one of the local clubs. It was one thing to talk to a good-looking guy who'd caught his interest and them not be interested. It was something else entirely to do the same thing and have to remember there was literally *no* chance of them ever being interested.

He needed to get a wider range of friends or something.

"I'll contact the other lawyer and the two owners," Lucas told him as he stopped at the door. "I'll find out what they have to say about the entire thing and either I'll contact you or they will."

"Sounds good," Dan told him, flashing a genuine smile. "And thank you for at least being willing to give this a try."

"Thank me if I take it on and see it through," Lucas told him. "Have a good rest of your evening."

"You too," Dan told him, waiting until Lucas was out of earshot before continuing. "Mr. Professional."

He grinned as he heard the sounds of the rest of the employees on the shift gathering out on the main floor. It wasn't often they had a new potential employee for everyone to gawk at, so Dan was sure they were all too eager to see the show. Personally, Dan had a good feeling about the entire thing.

And pushing the thought of the interesting man he couldn't touch out of his mind, he stepped out of the office to go see the show.

LUCAS

It wasn't until past office closing hours that Lucas finally managed to make his phone calls. The first had been to the lawyer, a Stephen West, but it had gone straight to the man's voice mail and Lucas had left a polite but not too descriptive message on the man's machine.

Following that had been a call to Jacob Masters, as it was the first one on the list and he would have to call Rico Morales as well anyway. That conversation had gone smoothly and quickly, if only because Masters wasn't all that invested in the day-to-day running of the club. In his mind, if Morales wanted to open up another club without Masters' approval and with his own funds, that was his business. Lucas had thanked him for his time and moved on to the next call.

Rico Morales was not quite as succinct. Within the first ten minutes of the conversation, the man had managed to regale him with a story about a drunk couple who had tried to pick him up the night before and then promptly puked on one another. This, Lucas was sure, was probably due to the fact that the man's attention span appeared to be as fragile as his sobriety since the man's words were slurring at the edges as he tried to remember what they were talking about.

"The attempt at purchasing a property in the town of Scotsdale to expand your business," Lucas reminded him patiently.

"Ah, right. Wait, the fuck you calling me for? Dan's there."

"Daniel Masterbaum is not the owner and without your consent cannot be involved in the proceedings."

Rico snorted harshly into the receiver. "Like hell he can't. Shit, Dan's probably the smartest and most capable fucker I've got in there right now. Can't keep it in his pants half the time, but he's got his shit together. Just let him take care of things because I'm thinkin' of taking another week or two to hang out here…Vegas is kinda nice."

Wary of another subject change coming, Lucas pushed ahead. "Well, I can certainly allow him to make decisions on your behalf, but unless you include him in the purchase legally, he can't sign anything binding or legal."

"Eh, let him deal with that. If there's anything I need to sign, he'll make sure I do it. Kid can't let anything go once he gets his teeth into something," Rico muttered, though Lucas couldn't tell if it was a complaint or a compliment.

"Well," Lucas said, weighing his options. "I would still feel more comfortable if we had something to show that you were legally handing this decision over to him. So, based on what you're telling me, I'll make sure he gets the proper paperwork and he can send it on to you."

"Sounds good. Oh yeah, and he's gonna be the one who knows anything about it. I've barely been involved. Seriously, there's a reason I put that horn dog in charge when

I'm not around. Never seen anyone who can keep the rest of those idiots in line."

Lucas had to admit he could almost see what the man was talking about. While he hadn't witnessed much about Dan, the man had seemed to have his head on straight and knew what he was doing.

At the very least, Lucas was sure the man was at least personally capable. Dan had possessed a natural self-confidence and assertive nature that Lucas could appreciate. He himself had always been more reserved and patient, but having been around Mateo and their mother for so long, there was no way he would have reached adulthood without having a good deal of respect for the capability of the more forward-thinking members of society.

"He tried hitting on you yet?" Rico asked with a chuckle.

Dan had, but Lucas hadn't been bothered by it. Nor did he really want to tell this strange man about that either. It rubbed him in just the wrong way for him to call Dan a horn dog, all while singing his praises. Maybe he just didn't know Morales enough to accept when he was teasing, which honestly made the most sense.

"He was courteous and helpful," Lucas told him, leaving out any mention of what was or wasn't said.

"Which means you're either being nice, or you aren't his type," Rico snorted. "Alright, just leave it up to Dan. He can yell at me if he wants to."

"I will call him and let him know. You have a good rest of your afternoon Mr. Morales," Lucas told him, remembering that it was still afternoon in Nevada.

With that done, he sent a quick message to Dan, letting him know that he'd spoken to both the other men and would be willing to have a sit down with Dan at some point in the near future to talk over things. Just as he set his phone down, a sharp knock on the door brought his head up.

"Hey," he told his friend. "What are you doing here?"

"Popping in to make sure you hadn't died at your desk," Samuel told him with a raised brow.

"Are you going to start giving me shit for working too much just like everyone else?" Lucas asked dryly.

"Huh. You know, if other people, especially more than one person, are saying the same thing, maybe there's some truth to it?" Samuel asked as he helped himself to one of the chairs across from Lucas's desk.

"That kind of thinking is what gets people sucked into death cults."

"Yes, come drink the Kool-Aid with us, Lucas. Or you know, have a life."

"Is this your way of inviting me over for another dinner?"

"It just might be."

Lucas smiled, knowing full well it was the truth. He and Samuel had been close friends for years, and he knew his friend about as well, if not better than Samuel knew him. Samuel wasn't the sort to give Lucas hell about something unless he was both deadly serious and also had at least a minor fix for the problem in mind. In this case, it was Lucas's lack of social life and a homemade meal offered up.

"And who will be doing the cooking this time?" Lucas asked.

"We'll be having steaks," Samuel said, then added, "Off the grill."

"Ah, so Caleb will be doing the cooking then," Lucas said, nodding. "Because you can't be trusted around an open flame."

"I set fire to the grill *one time* and no one lets me live it down," Samuel grumbled. "I swear, even when Caleb's using it, he won't let me near the damn thing. It's not like that grill wasn't needing to be thrown out anyway."

Lucas grunted, pretending like he was commiserating while they both knew he wasn't. If Samuel was being offered a chance to bitch about something, he was going to take it, especially if it was about his husband. Just as Lucas bore the gentle bullying of his family as a sign of affection, so too he recognized that Samuel bitching about his husband was a show of love. He wasn't quite sure *how* it worked, he just knew that it did.

"And I'm sure you endure such treatment with all the dignity and grace that we can expect from you," Lucas said, reaching over to power down his computer.

"Damn right," Samuel grumbled, winking at him. "Heading out?"

"Well, I'm hoping my current client, or rather, the client I'm helping as a favor to my brother, gets back to me. That way, I can do a quick little meet-up and go home for the night to get some rest," Lucas said with a shrug.

"It's a Friday night."

"And?"

"And you make good money. You're good-looking and single. If you've got the time, go out and mingle."

"Did you just rhyme at me?"

Samuel hesitated, then screwed his features up into a frown. "Huh. I guess I did. Kind of annoying, actually."

"A little," Lucas agreed.

Samuel shrugged, leaning back to kick his feet up onto the desk. "My point is, you should go out and have some fun for once. It's been ages."

"You know why. I've been so focused on work," Lucas

reminded him, reaching out to grab a pen from his cup holder and nudge his friend's feet from the desk.

Samuel allowed his feet to be pushed off and then promptly put them back on the desk. "I do, it's true. But once upon a time, you gave me some sage advice that I took to heart. Now it's my turn to do the same."

Lucas glared at the man's feet. "I'm beginning to regret giving you that advice if that's the case."

"Aw, that's a shame because now I have free reign to return the favor whenever I feel it's necessary," Samuel told him with a grin. "And guess what's happening now?"

"That was not what I intended."

"Luke."

"What?"

Samuel cocked his head and gave a soft smile. "What's the point of doing all this work, making all this money, getting ahead, if that's all you're going to do? There's a whole world out there, full of people and experiences that you're missing out on. Go enjoy yourself, have a little fun, do something that isn't sitting around dealing with other people's problems all the time."

"I distinctly remember a time when you weren't all that keen on going out and dealing with people or with doing things," Lucas said.

Samuel plopped his feet on the ground with a grin. "You're right, I didn't, and I was wrong. And if it wasn't for you and Caleb, I might not have learned that. So why don't you give it a try?"

"I have to be up early tomorrow for a meeting," Lucas told him, frowning.

"You don't on Sunday."

"And how would you know?"

"Because Alan has started worrying about you too and

was more than happy to give me your work schedule for the next few weeks so I could find a time to snag you for some socialization."

Lucas realized he should have known the secretary would be Samuel's source of information. The man was as efficient and organized as he was nosy and interfering. Lucas was going to have to find time to pull the man aside and tell him he shouldn't tell anyone his schedule, especially his most annoying friends.

Before he could say anything, his phone vibrated, alerting him to a message. He glanced down to see it was a message from Dan, telling him he still had time to stop in before the club opened if he wanted a quick chat.

Lucas sighed. "I'll take what you said into consideration."

"Like I don't know that means you're going to completely ignore everything I've just said," Samuel said with a roll of his eyes.

Lucas stood up. "I have paperwork I need to give to someone before I can go home and relax. So if you'll let me live my life in peace."

"Fat chance," Samuel said, standing up with a grin. "If only because I'm hoping that maybe you will take all this advice to heart and think about it a little."

"You and everyone else in my life apparently," Lucas grumbled as his friend saw himself out, still chuckling.

IT WAS ALMOST eight by the time he showed up at Nocturne, praying the place opened at nine. He wasn't in the mood to deal with too many people, not when he was looking forward to the comfort of his couch and the inevitable collapse onto his bed. As much as he had to begrudgingly admit, if Samuel of all people was telling him he was locking himself away too much, then it was a sign. He really didn't want to put it to the test.

The large man, whose name Lucas had never been told, let him in and down the hallway into the open area. Lucas had no idea what the club looked like lit up, but he imagined it was probably impressive. The dance floor piqued his curiosity more than anything, leaving him wondering why it looked like glass and was segmented into various squares. He had never asked his brother, though Mateo had sworn up and down the place was 'magic' when it was lit up and filled with people.

"Hey, you made it," Dan's familiar voice called from somewhere near the back.

Lucas turned and stopped as the other man jogged toward him. When they'd been introduced, Dan had been wearing a casual shirt and jeans combination, his hair flat against his skull as he'd poured over paperwork. Apparently, Dan didn't go into a business night looking quite as casual and Lucas had to remind himself that the man was a dancer by trade.

Though he'd never seen a male stripper in action before, he imagined that the skintight trunks the man was wearing would probably fit right into whatever dance he was working. They were snug, and as Dan turned to shout something down the nearby hallway, Lucas realized that they, in fact, fit the man like a second skin. They hugged the curve of the man's ass, leaving absolutely no question as to the size and shape.

Which was the point when Lucas realized what he was doing, quickly shook himself of the sudden distraction and focused on Dan's face.

"I did," Lucas told him, his throat a little dry, forcing him to clear it. "I spoke to Mr. Morales today."

Dan turned, his now loosely styled hair bobbing airily to fall down over his accented eyes. Lucas was struck by the realization that the hairstyle was probably supposed to emulate bedhead or sex hair and thought it worked pretty well. And it wasn't until Dan turned his head up into the nearby light to frown in confusion at Lucas that he saw the man's eyes had eyeliner.

"So your message told me," Dan told him, smiling now. "And Rico called me to ramble on about his conversation with you. Pretty sure he was drunk when he called."

"I had the same thought," Lucas said with a smile, noting that the line of black under the other man's eyes only drew attention to them. "I informed him he would have to sign a few pieces of paperwork to permit you to handle the situation in his stead."

"And Jacob?"

"This apparently is an endeavor that Mr. Morales is doing of his own accord with his own funds. So Mr. Masters will not be included."

"Oh. Rico never told me that, the asshole. The man leaves me in charge and then gives me the run-around."

Jacob reached into his suit jacket pocket and pulled out an enclosed thumb drive. "The paperwork you'll need him to sign is on here. I figured digital would be much easier for everyone involved."

Dan took it from him, their fingertips brushing. "Thanks. I'll get him to sign it when he sobers up some time tomorrow afternoon. I can promise you that."

"The sooner we settle this, the sooner we can get everything moving. Otherwise..." Lucas trailed off as Dan once again twisted to look at a noise behind him.

"Otherwise, we'll be waiting on Rico's ass to get anything done and we both know that isn't going to happen," Dan finished for him with a laugh, turning back toward Lucas.

At that moment, Lucas wanted nothing more than to be back in his house, where he could rest. Between losing the thread of conversation, getting distracted by the other man, and unable to think of what to say, he was clearly tired. All he needed was a good night's relaxation, followed by an even better night's rest.

Even if it *was* nice to talk to someone new, specifically someone who not only wasn't actively dragging down the mood but by dint of his personality actually managed to raise it up.

"On that note," Lucas said, feeling a little begrudging in what he was preparing to say. "I should probably head out."

Dan nodded, then his eyes widened. "Hey! I just had an idea."

Lucas hesitated and motioned to him. "Go on."

"I mean, you don't have to, but you've said you've never been in a place like this, right?"

"I don't think we've talked about that, actually. But otherwise, no."

"Huh. Must have been something Mateo said. Still, the point remains. Would you be interested?"

"These...aren't really my sorts of places," Lucas admitted, with less surety than he'd used when talking to others.

Dan shrugged. "Maybe not, but sometimes a place can seem that way until you give it a try. Hell, isn't that what Chris always used to say? And then BOOM, he ends up liking it."

"I think he enjoyed my brother a lot more," Lucas said dryly.

Dan laughed. "That's true, but hey, maybe you'll find someone you'll like a lot more than the dancing."

Lucas chuckled. "I can't imagine that will be the case."

"Hey, we have female dancers. Well, one now, but I've got another one interviewing next week."

"That wasn't quite what I meant."

Dan thought about that for a moment before nodding. "Well, if you change your mind, you can always come in tomorrow night. With me taking over for Rico, I'm not dancing like I was before, so I can keep you company and keep the worst people away from you."

Lucas hesitated again, knowing he should say no. He'd had many an invite to a strip club before, and half of them had been to Nocturne. The latter had been easy to turn down since there was no way in hell he wanted to watch his little brother shaking his dick around on stage for a bunch of drooling drunks. The former, well, he wasn't really someone who had an interest in strippers in general and honestly couldn't see the appeal.

"I'll think about it," Lucas said instead, realizing he meant it.

"Cool," Dan said, looking delighted even at that answer. "Just let me know. I'll put you on the VIP list so you can retreat to somewhere quiet that isn't the cluttered office."

"Sure," Lucas said.

"Yo, Dan! Michelle is losing her mind over her stupid tiara!" a voice cried from somewhere down the dark hallway behind Dan.

"I am not!" another yelled, high and furious.

Dan rolled his eyes. "I swear, strippers are either high maintenance or the calmest people."

"Which are you?" Lucas asked with a smirk.

Dan smiled up at him, then winked. "I guess you'll have to wait and find out."

With that, the other man spun on his heel with a wave, walking off toward the back where the sound of bickering was growing louder. Lucas watched him go, dedicatedly staring at the back of the man's head rather than anywhere else. Just as he made to walk away, Dan stopped at the doorway and turned to give him a cheery wave before disappearing into the darkness.

Waving back, Lucas made for the front door, wondering just how much sleep he'd been deprived of the past several weeks if one conversation with a relative stranger was knocking him so off-balance.

DAN

"Are you kidding me?" Dan complained as he stared down at his phone.

Beside him on the grassy patch, Max stirred. "What's up?"

Dan sighed, closing his phone and dropping it onto his lap. "One of the dancers isn't coming in tonight. Apparently caught a stomach bug. As if I don't know what that means."

Max chuckled, closing his eyes once more. "They found that bug at the bottom of a bottle."

Dan watched Max's nephew tear across the park, a ball under his arm. The kid wasn't even at the age of puberty yet, but Dan could see he was going to end up tall. Probably taller than he and Max both, which really wasn't saying much when it came to Dan. The handful of boys his age were quick on his heels, and Dan wasn't sure if they were trying to play football or just chasing whoever had the ball in the first place.

"Eh, I'd rather not have a hungover dancer in for the night anyway," Dan admitted. "But it puts me in a pickle."

"A pickle," Max repeated with a chuckle. "I don't think I've actually heard someone say that before."

"Might as well. I've had enough pickles in my mouth as it is."

"Not only did that barely make sense, but it was awful and you should feel ashamed."

"Maybe, but I don't."

"My friend Dan, without shame? What a strange occurrence."

Dan laughed, knowing it was true and taking a measure of pride in it. Not being too worried about what other people thought had made his life a great deal easier at times. It also made it incredibly easy to be a stripper, something he'd pointed out to people several times in the past.

"We have a new dancer," Dan explained. "I'm supposed to have someone bigger and more well known to headline, that way this Aidan guy can feel more comfortable on the stage. I don't need a newbie warming people up, ya know?"

He wasn't *that* much of a hard-ass with new dancers.

"Well," Max said, finally opening his eyes to look at him. "*You* are a more well-known dancer who's good at getting the crowd going."

Dan sighed. "I know. But I already invited you and Jacob to come out for the night, and I promised Lucas I wouldn't have to dance so I could pay attention if he did come out."

"That's the lawyer, isn't it?."

"That he is."

"You invited your lawyer to see a strip club."

"I invited him out to maybe see it for himself and try to have a fun night. Mateo always complained that his brother never got enough fun in his life and really, Lucas *is* pretty serious."

Max sat up to raise a brow at him. "Are you sure you didn't invite him out because you're interested in men in suits?"

Dan laughed. "I mean, I do like men in suits. And I like tall, buff, good-looking men in suits. Which, he is all those things. But he's straight, so I'm not going into this with an ulterior motive, I swear."

"Says the man who's already notched a few 'straight guys' on his bedpost," Max said, still watching him.

Dan shrugged. "Bi-curious isn't the same thing. Lucas is straight, even Mateo swears it."

"Yeah, because the man's brother is going to know whether or not he wants dick or not," Max said wryly.

Dan pushed him away with a laugh. "You *are* coming out, right?"

Max snorted, batting Dan's hands away. "Jacob said it sounded like fun, and it has been a little while since either of us got out. And since I've finally convinced Kayla that she doesn't have to work full-time *and* be a full-time student as well as a mom, she's going to be home with Collin."

"Oh boy, an uninhibited night for you two? I give it two hours at the absolute most before you're drunk and trying to feel him up in a dark corner and he ends up dragging you out of the club and banging you in the backseat."

"Hey! We can get an Uber."

"Sure, give the driver a show, why not?"

As Max chuckled, Dan felt his phone give a buzz. He looked down and saw a message from Lucas had arrived.

I've thought about your offer, and I realize I could probably use a night out. If it's still standing, that is.

Dan smiled.

Oh yeah it is ;)

Good. I'll be there shortly after nine if that works for you.

It does, see ya then

"That the lawyer?" Max asked, reclining back to loll his head and rest in the sunlight streaming down on them.

"Yeah," Dan said, tucking his phone away. "I guess I'm more persuasive than I thought. Because seriously, I thought he was going to text me and say no."

"And yet you were worried about him showing up anyway."

"Hey, I like to bank on hope but always acknowledge that something could go wrong."

"Practical of you."

Dan snorted. "I'll have to tell him the slight change of plans when he gets there tonight."

"Why not tell him now?"

"Eh. I don't want him to have an excuse to bail out, you know?"

"Uh-huh."

Dan rolled his eyes, purposefully ignoring the insinuation that Max was trying to make. In truth, he probably should have told Lucas that things had changed and that he would have to leave the man for a little bit. But the dance was at ten and he could keep Lucas entertained for the first hour, and his dance would last only about twenty minutes. Hopefully, Lucas wouldn't decide to bail the minute he learned the truth.

"So," Max said, still looking as comfortable as possible. "When are you planning to go back to school?"

Dan groaned. "When I'm not working the equivalent of two different full-time jobs?"

"You're only playing manager right now. You haven't been for the past few years since you dropped out."

"Fine, when I figure out what I want to do and not

while I'm building up a debt to the government as I figure it out."

He knew stripping wasn't going to be something he could do for the rest of his life. In fact, he knew that the time to quit was drawing closer. As good a shape as he was in, it was inevitable that time and age would have their way with him. Once his hair started thinning and it became nearly impossible to keep his stomach flat, he wasn't going to be very popular with the crowd of people craving the sight of virility dancing around on stage.

"Hey, after this, wanna go fill up on fat and sugar?" Dan asked.

"If we get ice cream with Collin, Kayla will personally murder us both."

"And she has to know...why?"

Max opened one of his eyes, then closed it after staring at Dan. "Sometimes, you are a wise man. Sometimes."

"WE ALL GOOD BACK THERE?" Dan asked Donna as the crowd began to grow around the dance floor.

The former dancer turned bartender popped up and gave him a wink. "We're all set. You can relax, no one wants to see a tense stripper."

Dan rolled his eyes. "Don't remind me."

The people were rolling in quickly, but that was to be expected. With a big strip show at ten and a smaller one at midnight, both Saturdays and Sundays, the club tended to fill up quickly. It was one way they managed to justify opening up a little later than the bars and other clubs in town did, and while Dan had heard the occasional complaint, he'd yet to see anyone kick up a fuss about it.

"You gonna mingle tonight?" Donna asked as she grabbed two beers for a couple of patrons.

"Yeah, I got people coming in who want to be social," Dan told her. "Just waiting on them to show up."

"Well, I'm guessing the cute guys waving at you right now are two of them," Donna said, pointing.

Sure enough, Jacob and Max were waiting for him off to the side and away from the crowd, where people were streaming in from the entrance. Dan waved at Donna as he went to meet them, grinning.

"You guys are earlier than I thought you'd be," Dan told them once he was close enough.

Max shrugged. "Jacob wanted to watch you shake your ass, so we made it in time for the first show."

Jacob rolled his eyes, bumping Max's shoulder gently. "What my boyfriend is trying to say is that he gets up brutally early to open his store personally almost every single day. So he wanted to come in so he could be drunk by midnight and go home."

"See, now that one..." Dan said, pointing toward Jacob, "sounds a lot more believable than whatever bullshit you just came up with. Twinks are *so* not his thing, so he's not here for me."

"Are you saying I'm not cute enough to be a twink?" Max asked with a raised brow.

"No," Jacob said with a smirk. "Or rather, you're not the twinky kind of cute. *I* think you're cute, though."

"I feel like I should be offended, but I'm not," Max said, shooting the man the look that Dan had started referring to as the 'gooey' one.

"Well, let's get you guys up to the VIP room with some drinks," Dan said, rolling his eyes as they practically cooed over one another.

"Where's your lawyer?" Max asked, smirking at Dan now.

"According to my phone," Dan said, pulling the buzzing device out to see a message from Glam. "At the front door."

"Lawyer?" Jacob asked with a curious frown.

"I'll explain while we get upstairs," Max told him with a laugh.

"You guys, uh, don't mind keeping him company for like, half an hour, do you? I promised he wouldn't be left on his own," Dan asked, sticking his bottom lip out for full effect.

"Does that actually work on people?" Jacob asked.

"We'll be more than happy to keep him company," Max said with a roll of his eyes.

"See?" Dan pointed at Max. "It totally works."

"That is *not* what made me say that," Max called to his back as Dan retreated toward the front door.

Dan was still grinning when he found Glam and Lucas waiting for him near the hallway. The traffic of people flowed around Glam's massive body like second nature, shielding Lucas from the crowd. The lawyer had foregone his suit and traded it in for a light blue button-up, the sleeves rolled up to his elbows. The man still wore what looked like dress-slacks, but a glance told Dan the man was wearing what looked like boots rather than dress shoes.

"Well," Dan said when he was close enough to be heard. "Don't you dress up nicely?"

Lucas looked down at himself. "Uh, I always dress up? This is dressing down."

Glam rolled his eyes, walking away now that Dan had a handle on the situation. Dan had a sneaking suspicion the man wasn't really all that worried about Lucas now he'd been there a few times around Dan and hadn't started any trouble. Dan had long since gotten used to Glam's extremely protective nature, especially for the smaller and admittedly more vulnerable members of the crew. He couldn't wait to see him start to play big brother with the new guy.

"That was the joke, Big Guy," Dan told him, almost reaching out to take Lucas by the hand but instead motioning for him to follow. "C'mon, let's get you a drink. You didn't drive, did you?"

"Uh, no. I got a ride here. Figured if I was going to go in on this, I might as well go all the way, right?" Lucas asked.

"Watch who you say that around," Dan told him as they approached the bar. "Especially dressed like that."

From the bewildered expression he caught on the man's face, Dan realized the other man had no idea what the hell Dan was talking about. Either Lucas had been out of the game for a long time, or unlike how he made it sound before, the man honestly had no idea how he looked. In Dan's opinion, it didn't matter if the man was wearing a suit or something more suitable for the club, Lucas made it look good.

And he'd bet good money the man looked just as good if not better in less.

"Hey, Donna," Dan said once the woman wasn't bent over grabbing something. "Get me a Virgin Special for my friend here."

"Give me one sec," she called back, sliding a glass along the bar to someone.

"Virgin Special?" Lucas asked curiously, speaking louder now that the music was growing in volume.

Dan nodded. "We have a drink here that Donna herself made up a few years ago. Tastes delicious and kicks like a mule. We give it to people who are clearly new here, and if we like ya, we give it out for free the first time."

Lucas blinked and then laughed. "Oh God, you weren't kidding about trying to get me to have a good time, were you?"

"Look, I might joke about a lot of things, but having a good time? That's not one of them," Dan promised as a tall drink and two large shot glasses were laid before him.

"Oh shit," Dan said as he eyed the shot glasses.

Donna tipped him a wink. "One Virgin Special, and two Danny Boy's."

Lucas squinted at the two large shot glasses. "And dare I ask?"

"Same principle as the drink," Dan told him, mouthing his thanks to Donna. "But a little less tasty because of the kick. Harder to hide it when it's so little."

"I knew I should have eaten closer to coming here," Lucas said, though Dan noted the man didn't seem to be regretting anything. "You're as bad as Mateo."

"Yeah, there was a contest to see whether his named shot was stronger than mine once," Dan said, handing over one of the shot glasses to Lucas.

"And what was the result," Lucas asked as he stared at the pearly white shot glass.

"Um, a tie," Dan said with a wrinkle of his nose. "A very messy tie."

Dan really did not want to think about how much puke both he and Mateo had produced that night. Nor did he ever want to think about the strangely tasting spicy but sugary drink the man had concocted that Dan swore contained stronger alcohol than was technically legal.

"Here's to your good night," Dan said, clinking their glasses together.

The liquor poured over his tongue and down his throat, coating both in the tangy and sweet flavors that made up the shot. He wasn't surprised when Lucas puckered for a moment after the shot went down, eyeing the glass apprehensively.

"Yeah, that's one reason why it was a messy tie," Dan said with a laugh, taking the man's shot glass and leaving both on the bar. "Because neither of our shots are meant to be drunk back to back."

"It's...very sour," Lucas noted with a slight wince.

Dan slid the tall glass into Dan's hand. "Drink this then. It's a little more on the sweet side, but not so much that you think you'd just eaten a tart."

Lucas took a drink, paused, and to Dan's delight took an even bigger second drink. "Okay, I'll admit, that is good. And *very* dangerous."

"Yeah," Dan drew out, watching Lucas take another sip. "You might wanna nurse that for a little bit, let the shot and those first couple of drinks get into your system. Or I might end up having sent you on your worst night in a while. No one wants to puke."

"Mmm, memories of college," Lucas said, shaking his head.

"Ooh, a secret party boy," Dan said with a laugh, enjoying as he watched Lucas's tense aura slowly fade as he looked around. "And Mateo made it sound like you were super responsible."

"You can be responsible and still get drunk at frat parties on the occasional weekend," Lucas said with a laugh. "And he should have mentioned that the last time he and I drank together, I drank him under the table."

"Oh?" Dan said, a little impressed. "I know how much Mateo can take. I'm a little surprised."

Lucas shook his head. "It was years ago. And I'm sure

between the drink I had before leaving and these ones, I'm going to be on my ass if I'm not careful."

Dan stopped and then let out a laugh. "You pre-gamed before showing up? God, it really has been years since you went out, hasn't it?"

"I'm still cool," Lucas told him, voice loud enough to hear and yet still somehow completely deadpan.

Dan chuckled and without thinking, grabbed Lucas by the wrist and pulled him toward the stairs leading up. "C'mon. I'll introduce you to a friend of mine and his boyfriend. You already talked to Jacob so at least you know one another."

"They come here together?" Lucas asked, following along willingly as they weaved through the crowd.

Dan waited until they got to the stairs, where it was a little quieter, before answering. "Sometimes they do. They usually come on nights when I'm not dancing, though. I think it weirds Max out to see me do my thing."

"Having avoided this place like the plague, especially while Mat was working here, I can't say I blame him," Lucas said as they reached the top of the stairs.

"Oh!" Dan said, spinning around and almost slamming into Lucas. He had to look up at the man, wincing apologetically. "Sorry. Actually, double sorry."

Lucas didn't move away, only raising a questioning brow. "Why double sorry?"

"Well, for almost bumping into you and also, despite what I said, I can't be your escort for the entire night. The lead dancer for the night called in sick today, and I'm going to have to take over for them. So there's going to be about thirty, maybe forty minutes where I'm not going to be around."

Lucas thought about that for a moment and then

nodded. "Hence why you're introducing me to your friends."

Dan shrugged. "If I can't be around to keep you company, I know they'll do it without a fuss. Plus, they're good people."

Max and Jacob were lounging on one of the plush benches that stood against the large windows looking out on the dance floor. Drinks sat before them on a small table, and they were talking quietly. Dan pulled Lucas over, introducing him to both of them.

It was amusing to watch as Lucas took Max's hand, smiling kindly and greeting him. The air took a slight shift, however, when it came time for Jacob and Lucas to interact. Almost immediately, the aura between them grew less casual and the two greeted each other warmly but carefully as they took one another's hands. It struck Dan that the two men were sizing one another up.

Max leaned in. "You catch that?"

"Lawyer and business tycoon. When worlds collide," Dan muttered with a snicker.

"Think they'll whip it out to see who's is bigger next?"

"Oh God, I'd pay to see that."

Max gave an ugly snort. "Like hell."

Jacob turned his attentive gaze on them, cocking his head. "And what are you two giggling about over there."

"I was not *giggling*," Max protested.

"You were," Dan told him, turning his amused gaze on Lucas. "And we were talking about you two."

"I'll admit," Lucas said, glancing between Max and Dan. "I'm a little afraid to ask about what."

"Good instincts," Jacob told him, eyeing them both as well. "Because when it comes to these two, it's never a good idea to ask."

"Don't lump me in with him," Max complained, swatting Jacob's chest.

Jacob laughed. "Babe, you're his friend...willingly, I might add."

"Oh, thanks," Dan said sarcastically. "You make it sound like such a hassle."

"Well," Max began but couldn't finish as he tried to get away from Dan who was trying to hop on his back.

Before he could enact his proper vengeance, a voice from the speaker system pierced through the music. "Ladies and gentleman, I hope you're ready for the night's big show. Just sit tight, enjoy your drinks, and wait while we get everyone ready. See you in fifteen minutes!"

"Ah fuck," Dan huffed, dropping from Max's back. "That would be my cue. You three behave yourselves, I'll be back soon."

Before he left, he gave a glance toward Lucas, who had situated himself next to Jacob but was talking comfortably with both. He seemed to have grown more animated since he first walked in, and Dan knew that the alcohol played a part in it, but he hoped maybe he was really just enjoying himself as well.

With that thought in mind, he left the trio, slipping into the mindset he needed to fully enjoy the upcoming dance.

LUCAS

Lucas was quickly realizing that he probably should have taken Dan's advice about his alcohol intake. He had only taken a couple of shots before leaving the house because of his sudden case of nerves. It had struck him as absurd. It wasn't as if he'd never gone out before, even if it felt as though it had been ages since the last time.

Yet those couple of shots, plus whatever the hell had been in the shot the bartender and Dan had given him, felt like it was going straight to his head. It didn't help that he had been sipping the drink he'd been given as well, though more out of nerves than anything else. He was relieved to find, however, that shortly after Dan left, he felt his nerves ease up, assuming that the alcohol was at least doing that much for him.

Max leaned back against Jacob on the cushioned bench. "Dan told me you've never been here before."

Lucas nodded. "I haven't been to any strip club. They've never really been my sort of place."

"Mm, a pity," Jacob said, glancing out toward the dance

floor which was emptying out so the strippers could use it. "Stripping is an interesting event to witness."

Max chuckled. "That might sound like a horny statement, but Jacob's a big fan of dancing in general. Doesn't matter what it is. Well, maybe it's a *little* horny."

Jacob kissed the top of Max's head fondly. "There's an irony in you accusing anyone of that."

Max turned to Lucas with big, round eyes. "Can you believe he's saying *this face* isn't innocent?"

Lucas cracked a small smile, shaking his head. "My soon-to-be brother-in-law has one of the most innocent faces and used to have one of the most innocent personalities."

"Used to have?" Max asked.

"Yes, until he met my brother. And now I've learned that nothing and no one that looks cute and innocent usually is," Lucas told him, much to Max's disappointment and Jacob's amusement.

"Damn it," Max grumbled, flopping back against Jacob's arm. "Even the straight boy knows."

Jacob looked up sharply for a moment, and Lucas thought he saw surprise ripple briefly across the man's face before it disappeared. Lucas had no idea what would have been so surprising about his sexuality. Was it because he was so comfortable around the couple? Or had Jacob assumed Dan was either with or trying to get with Lucas?

"Women can be quite adorable and seem innocent," Lucas told Max. "And having dated a few of them in my life, I can tell you they are usually anything but."

"Don't mind him," Jacob said, all traces of his reaction from before completely erased from his eyes. "He's just disappointed that someone else isn't falling for it."

"I suspect you fall for it a great deal," Lucas said with a smile, taking another drink.

"He so does," Max said, sounding proud of that fact.

Based on Jacob's rather put-together and reserved manner, Lucas expected the man to find a firm but still polite way of denying the charge. Instead, Jacob smiled fondly down at Max, patting his thigh.

Jacob shrugged. "When you're a sucker, you're a sucker. And I'm perfectly okay with that."

It reminded Lucas of watching Mateo and Christopher interact. At first, Lucas had been surprised to see how easily and quickly his brother had given in to Christopher, practically falling head over heels in the course of a few short weeks. It wasn't that Mateo wasn't normally affectionate and kind, but there was something different, warmer and brighter, about the way he'd been with Christopher. As if the quiet nerd had unearthed something in Mateo that no one but Christopher had known was there.

It was lovely to see, but it threatened to pull at a loose thread around the edges of Lucas's mind. As much as he could appreciate watching other people happy with one another, it only served to draw attention to the complete absence of the same in his own life. As much as he told himself, and believed for the most part, that he was perfectly fine on his own, it didn't change the fact that he was still prone to the twinges of loneliness.

Max turned as the lights outside grew darker. "Oh, they're starting. C'mon, Lucas, you might as well watch this. Even if you're not into guys or stripping, you still gotta see it at least once."

"And they do have a couple of women that perform here as well," Jacob said, turning in his seat to look down.

Lucas joined them, looking down to find all the lights save those on and above the stage turned off. Every panel on the dance floor was lit with a soft white glow, but he'd seen the way each panel could display a different color when he'd first come into Nocturne. It had certainly made for a colorful experience, and he was sure it wouldn't be any different when the dancers came on.

As the background music died down, something else took its place, much louder than the music before. It was high energy and slightly quirky, and Lucas had no idea who the singer was or what the song was called. Not that it surprised him, Mateo had always joked that Lucas had found one genre of music and had decided to camp there for the rest of his life. Even Lucas couldn't deny that.

Before he could think to ask what the song was supposed to be, however, a figure came out from the back of the stage. He knew it was Dan, but even he wasn't prepared for the sight of the other man. Dan's comfortable but trendy clothes had been replaced with a simple white dress shirt, buttoned all the way up and squeezing tight to Dan's chest and shoulders. Rather than simple slacks, however, the man wore a pair of black pants, shining and so tight looking that Lucas wondered how the man was managing to walk in them, let alone prepare to breathe.

Dan strolled out to the center of the stage, moving more like a runway model than a stripper. He looked around slowly, smiling in a perfect imitation of bemused curiosity, as if wondering what everyone was doing out there, watching him. He reached up, adjusted the knot on his tie, almost unconsciously.

And then the music shifted immediately, the beat dropping low and thrumming through the speakers. In perfect sync with the music, Dan began to move, his body coming alive with the music. It twisted and turned, moving with a grace Lucas would have never guessed the man possessed.

"He's such a show-off," Max said with a laugh as Dan

grew closer to the crowd, getting almost within touching range before backing off.

"You have to admit that he has skill, though," Jacob said, cocking his head.

"Yeah, but that would just go straight to his head, so you're not allowed to tell him I said so."

Lucas barely heard a word of the conversation as Dan's body continued to cavort from one end of the stage and to the other. Cavort was the best word he could think of as he watched the man playfully work the crowd. There wasn't a moment's hesitation or doubt, with Dan moving in perfect confidence as he blended together playful coyness and confident teasing.

It was like watching the man play a game where he made up all the rules.

Despite his earlier protests, Lucas found himself absolutely engrossed in the show. Dan managed every twist of his body, every shift of his hips as though it were second nature. In his mind, there was no way anyone could watch the show and not at least be impressed.

As the music shifted to another song, one Lucas barely paid attention to, the first few buttons of Dan's shirt came undone. Lucas hadn't even seen the man undo the buttons and faintly wondered how he'd managed that little magic trick. It happened again and again until finally the shirt was open and Dan's chest and stomach were on display, just in time for him to arch his back and show the ripple of muscles along his entire midsection.

Dan's hand ran down the middle of his chest, across his stomach and came to rest on his waist. A thrust of his hips and suddenly the pants were undone, revealing a shock of crimson. Still smiling that knowing yet playful smile, Dan turned from the crowd, his hips shifting just enough for his pants to slide down slightly, revealing more of his red underwear.

Lucas swallowed as the shirt shifted backward, sliding down Dan's sinewy arms and dropping to the floor of the stage. Dan wasn't bulky, but it was obvious he took care of his body as the muscles shifted beneath sweat-shining skin. He turned to face the crowd once more, hips pushing forward as the open flap of his skin-tight pants showed the crotch of his underwear, his hand coming down to playfully cup himself.

"He's in rare form tonight," Max noted, peering down at the stage. "Normally, he's not this…"

"Horny?" Jacob supplied.

"Yeah, that. Nice of you to notice."

"You noticed too."

"Gross."

The pants were lost next as the song shifted, but they weren't simply kicked off. Instead, Dan took his time inching them down his body, first letting the sway of his body move them further down his hips and then finally hooking his thumbs into the waistline to pull them down further. As they slid down the curve of the man's ass, Lucas was reminded of the shape it had made in the underwear he'd seen him in the night before. His heart stuttered in his chest as Dan arched his back again, pushing his ass toward the crowd as his pants dropped to his ankles.

There was only the thin and skintight pair of bright red underwear keeping Dan from being completely revealed to the entire crowd. Even from the VIP room, Lucas could see the dips in Dan's stomach, lines that drew the eye's attention to the man's groin. Dan twisted again, his ass on display as he did everything to move his body in a way that accentuated the entire thing.

And before he knew it, the music began to dwindle away and Dan grinned, striking a pose and waving to the crowd. He gathered up his clothes from the stage, gave a cheeky wave to the audience once more and disappeared into the back.

Lucas turned from the stage, even as the music began to shift once more, signaling the next dancer. The dance was everything that people swore stripping was supposed to be, and even then, Lucas had not been prepared for what he'd witnessed. He could see, on a certain intellectual level, why Jacob found it so amusing to watch. There was a grace and skill required to look somehow both elegant and sensual at the same time. It required walking a thin line that could easily be overstepped with the slightest mistake.

Yet, Lucas knew full well that Dan had managed it completely, perhaps even flawlessly. Ignoring that he would have never predicted he'd be knocked off balance by a stripper, he certainly never expected a *male* stripper to impress him. Lucas had found himself riveted by the entire twenty-minute dance, enthralled as Dan worked him as surely as he worked the crowd. His eyes had been drawn by the man's movement, and probably intent, to different parts of his body, unable to look away as more and more of Dan was put on display.

"Oh, I haven't seen this one before," Max said, still watching the stage. "She must be new. That or it's been a while since I was in here."

"It has been a while," Jacob told him distantly. "Because I haven't seen her before either."

"I'm interested to see the new guy. Dan told me he's surprisingly good," Max commented, sounding intrigued.

Vaguely, he realized his mouth and throat were dry. Without thinking, he brought the tall glass to his lips and downed the rest of his drink in several heavy gulps. It slid down his throat easily, his stomach burning at the sudden rush of alcohol. He welcomed the sensation, though, hoping it would flood his system and drown out his overactive brain.

Yet, it wouldn't require alcohol for him to realize he had zero interest in whatever was happening on the stage anymore. He had been completely blown away by Dan's performance, and Lucas couldn't pretend it was purely intellectual. His heart was still thumping away in his chest, his stomach felt like it was doing somersaults, and he was thankful the VIP room was dimly lit. Otherwise, someone else might have noticed that his pants were fitting a lot more snugly than they had been twenty minutes before.

He had been turned on by Dan, and he had no idea how to even begin to process that information.

Lucas looked up as the server swung by once more, holding up a finger and a smile. "Another one of the Virgin Specials...if the nice woman at the bar is willing to make me one."

DAN

Dan could have easily left the dressing room after his show was over, but he lingered for the rest of the show. Mostly, he wanted to watch Aidan as he put on his first real show. Saturdays were generally easier days to put on a show for someone new. Fewer people came in, though it was still a sizeable enough crowd to make sure it counted. The crowd wasn't coming fresh off a long week either, more at ease and comfortable after having at least a day to unwind, and were more forgiving because of it.

Dan wasn't surprised to find that Aidan absolutely nailed his first performance. His instinct about the man had been dead-on when he'd seen him put on his show for the entire staff the week before. And he was delighted to find Aidan hadn't lost any of the charm or enthusiasm he'd had then. The man was a natural, and with a little more training, would develop and hone his own style that Dan could easily see making him the new top spot for customers.

"You know," Rebecca said, leaning against the door to the stage and watching Aidan wrap up. "When I started here last year, you made a comment about how you were going to have to retire soon."

Dan chuckled. "And that's still true. Time doesn't go backward, and no one wants to see a middle-aged balding man shaking it on the stage."

She grinned. "I don't know, you could have a dad bod night. I bet it would work."

Dan laughed at the idea. "You go ahead and tell Rico that one, see how well it works out."

"My point," she said with a smirk. "Was that I was kind of hoping it would give me a chance to be the headliner."

"You still could," he pointed out.

"Nah, not like you are. And now I'm watching this one...and I'm not going to make it to the front of the show bill anytime soon."

"My friend Mateo used to work here. He loved going last. Said it was more fun when the crowd was already hyped up but feeling a little full. Thought it was a challenge to get them revved up all over again instead of letting them get lazy."

"I saw his act a few times back in the day. That man had a gift."

"He did."

And that man who had once been the biggest name at Nocturne had turned around and settled down. He was living with Christopher, had finished his schooling, and was working his way to being a full-time, accredited therapist. Mateo had even confided in him that the two had talked about possibly having kids sometime in the future, though they hadn't decided exactly how. Dan could all too easily imagine the duo as great parents, and while he didn't want to have kids of his own ever, part of him ached to have someone he could at least consider being a co-parent with.

When Aidan finally finished up, he made his way to the back where Rebecca and Dan were waiting for him, both grinning widely. The younger man was covered in sweat, his red hair sticking to his forehead as he all but threw himself into the privacy of the back room.

"Nicely done," Dan told him, tossing him a towel. "I told you you'd have them eating out of the palm of your hand in no time."

Aidan accepted the towel with a grateful smile, wiping his face. "Thanks. That was...intense. I knew it was going to be different than musicals and plays, but damn."

Dan chuckled, patting the man on the shoulder. "And eventually, you'll figure out if it's a good intense or not. For now, go get yourself showered off and we'll get a drink back to you so you can unwind. If you want to go out and mingle among the crowd, be my guest, but make sure to keep security in your sights at all times."

They hadn't had any incidents since the stalker, but no one wanted to take that chance either.

Once he was sure that Aidan was alright and had been given the right amount of praise, he left him in the backroom to check on everything else before going up to the VIP room. Glam informed him that everything was sound on the security front, with only a couple of people being made to leave for getting too drunk and too handsy. That was sadly normal for the weekend, and Dan moved on.

"Your boy got himself another drink," Donna told him after he checked in with her.

"Oh yeah? Anything fun?" Dan asked as he waited for his own drink to be mixed.

Donna snorted, sliding his cocktail to him. "Yeah, another Special. I think he's looking to get wasted at this rate."

"Oh lord, I told him to watch those," Dan said with a groan. "We're going to have to roll him out of here."

Donna laughed. "Probably, but that's your problem...unless it becomes Glam's problem."

"It won't," Dan assured her with a frown, taking his glass. "You good here?"

"Yes, Mom, thank you."

Dan gave her the finger, making her laugh again as he walked away. While he knew everyone was well within their right to want to make sure that someone getting drunk didn't cause any trouble, he didn't like the idea of it being thrown Lucas's way. The guy might seem a little stiff and uptight, but Dan thought all he needed was to loosen up and enjoy himself. Then again, from the sounds of it, he wasn't having much trouble with that while he was left unsupervised.

Thankfully, most of the crowd didn't notice him or kept their conversation to a minimum as Dan tried to make his way upstairs. When dancers did their thing at Nocturne, they could either go out and mingle with the group or hide, much like Rebecca preferred. Some people just liked to show off and then never have to deal with the people on an individual level. While others, like Dan and Mateo, weren't exactly shy about going out to bask in the attention of their audience.

"Sorry," Dan proclaimed when he finally got to the VIP room. "Had a few people try to talk me up."

Max looked up from his conversation with Lucas and Jacob, grinning. "How many people asked to 'see you in private' tonight?"

"Miraculously, only a couple. Must be new here, because by now all the regulars know that I'm not going to just hand out private dances," Dan said.

Lucas eyed him, gaze sweeping over Dan's body. "Why's that?"

Dan almost made a move to check himself out as well, wondering what was wrong with what he was wearing. He'd thrown his performance clothes into the hamper used for the stripper's outfits to be laundered on Monday. After rinsing the sweat off, he'd returned to his previous set of clothes and no one had paid any attention.

Dan shrugged. "I'm just not a big fan of getting into a small room with people I barely know and letting them...well, do whatever."

Max turned his attention to Lucas, smiling in a way that hinted at a secret. "See, when people get a private dance, the rules get a lot more...loose in there. Both people talk it out first to figure out what's going to go on, but generally, someone's dick is out."

"He missed his calling as a writer," Jacob informed them as he took a drink.

Max grinned. "And sometimes...more happens."

"More?" Lucas repeated, turning his attention to Dan.

Dan shrugged, flopping down onto the bench beside him. "It's been known to happen. Generally, though, the strippers know that's what someone wants and they negotiate. That's usually the priciest lap dance you could ever hope to have too, at least here."

"Of course, they only charge for the dance itself," Max explained, glancing at Jacob. "Because if you decide to do something in private that's sexual, but only charge for the dance, then it's not prostitution."

"Ah, how familiar that sounds," Jacob said with a smirk.

"Escorts do the same thing," Dan explained, pointing at Max. "Which that little devil was before he went and shacked up with Jacob."

Max shrugged, bringing his straw to his lips and taking a drink. "The pay isn't nearly as good this way, but damned if the sex isn't better."

"I'd be insulted if I wasn't flattered," Jacob told him, giving Max's leg a squeeze.

Dan rolled his eyes, nodding toward the two of them as he spoke to Lucas. "And now begins the part of the night where Max starts getting tipsy and incredibly hands-on. Jacob will try to behave himself, but because he can't help himself, he'll give in and they'll be all over each other until someone drags the other one out of the club and we'll not see them again for the rest of the night."

Lucas chuckled, taking a sip of his own. "They were behaving themselves before you showed up. Maybe it's your presence."

Max blanched. "Oh God. Please don't make it sound like I get horny when Dan is around."

Jacob glanced at Dan, looking him over. "I don't know..."

"Jacob!" Max protested, swatting the man and making him laugh.

"This is flirting," Dan told Lucas. "Believe it or not, this is flirting for them."

Lucas smiled. "I think it's sweet. Neither of them are bothered or get jealous, they're comfortable with one another."

Despite how much the man had knocked back already, Lucas was incredibly sober sounding. Not one syllable was hesitated on or slurred. His gaze was less sharp, and his smile was a little looser, but without prior knowledge, Dan would have assumed the man had only had a few drinks. Apparently, being able to drink was a family trait.

"So, what'd you think of the show? Rebecca was probably fun to watch, right?" Dan asked, suddenly curious.

To his surprise and amusement, a flush of color rose to Lucas's face. "Ah, uh, Rebecca?"

Max leaned forward, smirking. "You know...the female dancer that came on after Dan."

Jacob rolled his eyes, nudging Max. "They introduced her as Diamond."

Dan laughed. "I told her that was the most stripper name under the sun and she told me that was exactly the point. I swear, I'm never going to understand her."

"Ah," Lucas said in realization and then nodded. "The dancing was...certainly not what I was expecting."

"Is that a good thing?" Dan asked with a raised brow.

"I'd certainly say it was good," Max said, now grinning to the point that Dan was tempted to ask him how much he'd had to drink.

Lucas cleared his throat, suddenly looking nervous, the expression foreign on the man's face. "I wasn't expecting it to be so interesting, I'll give you that. I can understand what Mr...Jacob was talking about shortly after you left. There is a great deal of skill involved in the dancing you do."

Dan beamed at the compliment. "Well, thank you, I'm glad you enjoyed it."

Lucas turned abruptly to Max and Jacob. "Dan tells me you two met in a rather...unique way."

Max laughed. "Oh yeah. The age-old tale of the rich man falling in love with a hooker. Gets 'em every time."

"You," Jacob began and then shook his head. "Never mind. Doesn't matter how many times I try to stop you, you always plow right on."

"I thought that was your job?" Max asked innocently.

"How much has he had to drink?" Dan asked with a wrinkled nose.

"Enough," Jacob told him.

Which didn't stop Max in the slightest from launching into the story. Dan was already well familiar with it and found himself distracted. Normally, it would be the number of tasks still waiting for him in the club before the end of the night. Instead, he found himself paying attention to Lucas, who was being polite and listening to Max's story with intense fascination.

He also noticed how close they were and how much heat was radiating off Lucas. Dan had never been able to explain it, but he'd always been fond of naturally warm men. There was something pleasing about their body heat against his. More than once, he'd found himself realizing that someone was warm, only for it to immediately flip a switch in his brain and his hands would start roaming.

There was no denying that Lucas was a good-looking man, and Dan would have happily flirted with him given the chance. Yet, even with the allure of the man's body, Dan had to admit he was quickly growing fond of Lucas. They barely knew one another, but there was an allure to the quiet nature of the other man and how absolutely steady he was in every situation Dan had seen him in.

Dan had a tendency to bounce around erratically, sometimes in a flurry of joy, and other times an absolute bundle of taut nerves. There was a comfort in being around someone who seemed to steadily work his way through life, even if it did come at the expense of his personal life. Dan remembered Mateo talking about Lucas, and his chief complaint was that the man was *too* dedicated to working hard and had a tendency to sacrifice himself in the process.

"It was all very Pretty Woman," Max concluded, taking a big drink.

"You are no Julia Roberts," Dan informed him.

"Nope, even better."

"How modest."

"The pot says to the kettle, calling him black."

Jacob shook his head, looking to Lucas. "There's not a trace of humility in either of them, trust me."

Lucas looked over at Dan, an amused twinkle in his eye. "Perhaps not, but that doesn't have to be a bad thing. The confidence to walk into the storm is the same one that gets people ahead in life."

Max squinted at Lucas's drink. "Just what are they putting in the cocktails nowadays? Because I want whatever he's having."

"I'm not that drunk," Lucas said with a laugh. "Just drunk enough and tired enough to feel a little philosophical."

Dan frowned at Max. "Leave the man alone. If he wants to recite whatever pops into his head, let him."

Max winked at him. "Whatever you say, boss."

"Someone," Jacob said slowly. "Is deciding to be a little shit tonight. Not that I should be surprised."

"Oh, am I going to be punished?" Max asked.

"C'mon," Dan said, pulling Lucas up with him. "Once Max starts getting flirty, it all goes downhill from there."

Lucas chuckled but didn't resist Dan's pull, going with him willingly. It was the second time Dan had taken hold of a situation and pulled Lucas along for the ride. It had always been something other men had complained about. Oh sure, they liked it at first, especially when it came time for the bedroom, but inevitably, they found it tiresome and annoying. Not that he had to worry about that with Lucas in general, but he still felt a small twinge of guilt at pulling the man around everywhere.

"Tell me they were better behaved when I left you with them," Dan pleaded once they were out of the booth. They were out on the balcony overlooking the dance floor, and Dan had to shout to be heard over the thundering music.

Lucas nodded. "They were perfect babysitters."

"They weren't babysitters," Dan protested.

"You assigned them to keep an eye on me so I wasn't left alone. Either because you didn't want me to get into trouble, or you didn't want trouble to find me."

Dan grinned. "Alright, when you put it like that, I can't exactly deny it, now can I?"

Lucas chuckled, leaning on the balcony's railing. "I don't mind. What's the point of going out if you're not going to enjoy a little bit of socialization? It's been so long since I last went out and just...enjoyed being around other people. I thought I was perfectly fine with that, but it's funny how you can just get used to something without realizing it. Not quite the same thing as being okay with it."

There was no denying that. Dan had been thinking something very similar only moments before when he'd been contemplating his own bachelor status in the backroom. Dan had grown used to being single, alone, and in a way, he was okay with it, as he would rather be alone than be with someone who wasn't right for him. But acceptance was something altogether different, and he wasn't quite ready to accept that he might not find that person.

"It's funny," Dan said, leaning next to Lucas so he wouldn't have to yell. "I was thinking the same thing earlier. But it was about the fact that I'm single and have been for a while now."

Lucas gave a crooked grin at that, and Dan realized that

was probably his truest smile. "I know the feeling all too well. Everyone in my life has been so worried about whether or not I'm getting out enough and if I'm dating. I keep telling everyone that I'm fine the way I am, and I'm doing what I want."

Dan nodded. "Same. But it doesn't mean that sometimes I don't want to have something more too, you know? It's nice...having someone to spend your days with, to know they'll be there at the end of the night."

Lucas glanced at him. "Forgive me if this is too much, but...I have a hard time understanding how you haven't been claimed by someone by now. You're obviously liked by people, and if the audience was any indication, you're obviously someone to be desired. You have a good head on your shoulders, and you're an optimistic and joyful person."

Dan glanced at him, smiling a little shyly. "Thank you, Lucas. It's nice to get a little boost every once in a while. And I know it seems silly to say since I barely know you, but I think you would make someone pretty happy yourself."

Lucas chuckled, shaking his head. "I'm told that I'm too distant and anally retentive. So, there aren't too many people clamoring to stay with me."

Dan grinned. "And people have called me flighty and irritating. Just because people see us one way doesn't mean we *have* to be that way. We can be whoever the hell we want and not have to worry about what a bunch of negative people think."

"And if people are right? And some things about yourself are wrong?"

"You decide that, not other people. If I listened to everyone else, I wouldn't be all the things you say I am. And you might not be the steadfast, even-keeled person you are, the very same thing I like about you."

He realized then that Lucas was drawing closer to him. Dan looked up in time for Lucas to cup his face, his fingers curling around the back of his neck. Shocked, Dan tensed, his eyes going wide as Lucas leaned in closer to him. Their mouths grew close enough that Dan could feel the warmth of Lucas's breath gusting against his lips. They brushed, and Dan felt a tingle rush through him, sending his heart into a frantic hammering.

And then, without warning, Lucas lurched back away from him, eyes huge.

"I need to go home," Lucas spat out, taking another step back from Dan. "It's already late."

The sudden shift in mood had Dan's head spinning, and he was already off-balance from the near kiss as it was.

"I'll message you when everything is in order," Lucas babbled, clearing his throat roughly. "Just make sure to send on the paperwork I provided so we can get follow through without any potential trouble in the future."

"Lucas?" Dan finally said, finding his tongue.

Lucas flashed him a smile. "Thank you for bringing me here. It was fun. And I meant it, the dance really was...something."

Dan could only stand, staring in confusion as Lucas took to the stairs and disappeared into the crowd. It wasn't until he saw the man disappearing out of the exit and it was too late to try and stop him that he realized he should have tried to stop Lucas. If only to figure out exactly where *that* had come from.

LUCAS

It had been a full work week before Lucas finally found the courage to pick up the phone and call Dan. From the moment he'd hit the street, the warm summer night air hitting his face, Lucas had felt his stomach twist. Whether it was with guilt, shame, or anxiety, he had no idea. He had *never* felt such a potent combination of awful emotions after trying to kiss someone before, and he didn't know what to do with it.

Then again, it was the first time he'd ever tried to kiss a guy.

When Monday had rolled around, Lucas had thrown himself into whatever he could find that would keep him busy. When the pile of things to do grew gradually smaller, Lucas realized he had no choice but to continue with the favor he was doing for Nocturne. Dan had already sent along the paperwork, dutifully signed and dated by Rico Morales, which meant he had no excuse not to set up some meetings.

He had silently hoped that Dan wouldn't answer, but he did when Lucas finally called him on Friday afternoon.

"Hey," Dan said, sounding like his normal self.

"Hey," Lucas said, having to clear his throat again. "All the paperwork you sent over is in order. I can set up an arrangement with the realty agency in charge of the building your boss is looking to buy."

"You'll probably need me there, won't you?" Dan said, sounding thoughtful.

Lucas couldn't tell if the man sounded upset about that or not. In all honesty, he wouldn't have blamed the man if he didn't want Lucas around him. Without any warning whatsoever, Lucas had almost forced himself on the other man. He'd made it very clear what his sexuality was, and Dan had respected that. Then, in a fleeting moment of some strange surge of attraction after one little dance, Lucas had completely lost his head.

"Well, I can represent you. But when it comes down to it, you're going to need to be the eyes and ears that know whether or not the location is going to work. In the notes you included, you said that neither you nor Mr. Morales had been on location."

"Yeah," Dan grunted. "We've been trying to do this with the help of a lawyer. But obviously, that's been uh...trying."

Lucas winced. "Undoubtedly."

"When were you thinking of having the meeting?" Dan asked.

Lucas looked over his schedule and hummed. "Well, it would probably be best if we had it somewhere in the middle of the week. I know your weekends are pretty busy. And the latest we could probably push an appointment with the agency would be somewhere around four, maybe five if I asked nicely."

Dan chuckled, the sound making Lucas smile. "I didn't know lawyers could ask nicely."

"We can on occasion. It generally makes you more friends," Lucas told him.

"Well, Tuesday would probably work best. And anywhere between two and four. If that doesn't work for them, just let me know?"

"I can do that."

"Awesome. I'll make sure to be conscious and ready to go by then. Do you want to meet out there or carpool?"

"Well, unless you have any other arrangements, we can take my car. We're going to the same place after all," Lucas told him, comfortably falling into the rhythm of a nice, normal conversation.

"Sounds good."

"Then I'll let you know what's going on when I know what's going on."

Dan hummed thoughtfully. "I'll be around. Lord knows I can't leave this phone anywhere or the world would collapse as I know it. So I'll talk to you later?"

"As soon as I know anything."

"Great. And when we carpool, you and I can talk about what happened at Nocturne."

The line clicked off before Lucas could do more than let his mouth fall open in surprise. If he hadn't been witness to it, he would have been surprised at just how casually Dan had dropped that final rejoinder before dropping the call. And if he didn't know any better, he would be suspicious that Dan had purposefully let the conversation go on as though nothing strange had happened between them before dropping his bombshell.

The more he thought about it, the more he realized that

probably was the case and that Dan was a lot more wicked than he might have originally given the man credit for.

Not sure if he was impressed, annoyed, or intrigued, Lucas busied himself with finding the number for the realty agency so he could set up the meeting. Finding the number, he called the agency's office, wondering if he wanted someone to answer and then wondering if he wanted them to have an open space on Tuesday afternoon.

The decision was made for him as a smooth male voice answered.

"Morning Down Realty, this is Michael."

"Hello," Lucas said, introducing himself. "I'm calling on behalf of Rico Morales, who is seeking an industrial-style project in Scotsdale."

"Ah yes," Michael said to the sound of clicking keys in the background. "I believe someone else is currently taking over the sale?"

"Yes," Lucas said, checking his notes. "A Daniel Masterbaum. He's currently seeking a viewing of the property."

"Well, you have good timing. I was just getting ready to leave. Is that too soon?"

"Ah yes, he was hoping for this upcoming Tuesday. Preferably in the early to mid-afternoon if that's doable."

"I don't see why not. We haven't had a lot of business this past month so our schedules are pretty open. Let me check."

There was a brief moment of pleasure at managing to catch the man and arrange the meeting. Lucas always enjoyed it when he managed to get something done, even the smallest of tasks. There was a thrill in a task well done, it didn't matter if it was something routine or not. Often, he suspected that was how he managed to get through the drudgery that was his workload while others tended to wallow in the tedium.

It didn't last long. Almost immediately, he realized he'd all but arranged for him to be stuck in a car with Dan and whatever the man had in store for him. He had no idea how Dan was going to react after Lucas's epic stumble at Nocturne. He also had no clue what the hell he was going to say to the man.

Sorry I tried to kiss you? I've never been attracted to another guy in my life but watching you on stage made me wonder what it would be like to have you naked beneath me?

The sentence in his head was enough to make him cringe, and to his bemusement, shift to get more comfortable in his pants. He could be bold when he wanted, and he could even be what some would call crass when he was alone with a trusted partner. All those partners had been women, however, and there had never been the slightest blip on his radar in the past that would even hint that he might be remotely attracted to other men.

"Still there?" Michael asked, breaking through Lucas's thoughts.

Or rather, his fantasies, considering his mind was more than happy to drift to the reminder of the curve of Dan's ass. Or the way the man had moved with a perfect, sensual grace...

"Yes," Lucas said quickly, clearing his throat roughly.

And he was most definitely not hard as a rock in his pants thinking about Dan while on the phone with a stranger, definitely not.

"Well, the afternoon is open. Do you have a specific time in mind?"

"He asked for a time between two and four, so let's go with two. Just to give enough time for wiggle room."

Another moment of clicking and then, "Right, well, we'll have one of our realty agents meet you out there at two. Is there anything else?"

Other than a burning desire to see a man naked for the first time in his life? "No, there's nothing else. Thank you for the help. I'm sure you're ready to get home."

Michael chuckled. "No problem, have yourself a nice day."

"You as well," Lucas said, ending the call.

Still unsettled by his wayward thoughts and his own body, he stared down at his phone. After a moment, he had the sense to message Dan and let him know the meeting was on at two.

A heartbeat later, and he opened the browser on his phone. Porn wasn't his favorite thing in the world, but it would do in a pinch if he really needed it. No one walked into his office without knocking, and the door was closed. So long as he kept the volume down, he'd be perfectly safe from any unnecessary intrusion.

After a few minutes of browsing, he found a perfectly good video. Sure enough, when the action got started, Lucas felt a familiar stirring in his pants. The woman in the video was more than enough to pique his interest, especially since it had been days since he'd last taken care of himself. He admired the curves of her body, watching her partner run his hands down her hips and over her thighs.

A sudden urge popped into his head, and once more, he considered his surroundings. Telling himself he was safe, he undid the buttons and zipper to his work slacks. Pushing his hand beneath the waistband of his pants and underwear, he gripped his cock.

His heart began to hammer as he stroked himself, knowing he could make it fast but wanting to at least take a couple of minutes. Lucas had never done *anything* at the office before, but pent-up arousal was taking over his rational thought. He watched the couple fuck on the screen, fingers gliding over the length of his cock and praying no one decided to break the unspoken rule of the office and just stroll in.

When the actor's hand slipped around to curve behind the woman's ass, using it as leverage for his thrusts, Lucas's thoughts stepped sideways. It had been Dan's ass, clothed in a tight pair of underwear, that had first snagged Lucas's attention. Then it had most definitely held his gaze while Dan was on stage, and from the performance, the other man definitely knew the asset he was working with and was not afraid in the slightest to show it off either.

His cock throbbed in his hand, growing sensitive and throwing a wave of pleasure through him. Lucas managed to stifle his low gasp at the sudden sensation, feeling himself tip over the edge. The video on the screen was a blur, his mind fixated on the image of Dan's ass, barely covered and wonderfully curved. Lucas held back his moan, releasing into his other hand as his thoughts drifted to wondering what it would be like to see the man's ass naked, spread out before him and...

Lucas let out a low gasp as the sudden ecstasy left him, clearing his thoughts. He had set out to prove that heterosexual sex was still what he was into, and that was most certainly true. Yet along the way, he'd stumbled upon the fact that he could just as easily think about a guy's ass and be just as interested.

He looked at his cum-covered hand and grimaced, okay, more than just interested.

Drawing his energy back, he used his clean hand to fish out the wipes he kept in the bottom drawer and cleaned himself up. As he settled down to try to focus on work, he realized there was absolutely no way that his steadily building realizations weren't going to be stuck in his thoughts for the next few days. And while he had no way to stop it completely, he knew he could at least stem the flow a little by keeping himself occupied for the next seventy-two hours.

Through work, work, and even more work.

Well, after he washed his hands anyway.

WHEN TUESDAY AFTERNOON FINALLY ARRIVED, Lucas was both surprised and a little disappointed when Dan slipped into the passenger seat and slumped into near-total silence. It wasn't until they stopped to get gas, and Dan emerged from the gas station with what Lucas thought was the biggest cup in existence full of steaming hot coffee that he realized what was wrong with him.

"Late night?" Lucas asked politely as he pulled out of the station.

"Always," Dan grunted, taking a tentative sip of the strong-smelling brew.

Except for nights where he'd stayed up far too late or woken up hungover, Lucas had never been sluggish in the mornings. He wasn't perky, which spared him the wrath of people who were grumpy in the morning, but he tended to wake quickly and go about his morning routine easily and smoothly. But he'd dealt with enough non-morning people to know to leave Dan alone as the man settled into his coffee and let the minutes tick by and the caffeine enter his bloodstream.

They were nearly a half-hour away from Scotsdale before he started seeing signs of life out of Dan. The man had been steadily drinking the coffee at a speed Lucas had found a little worrying at first. Yet he couldn't deny, as Dan started paying attention to the surroundings outside the car, began to fidget, check his phone, and make soft sounds of thought, that it was apparently working.

"It always feels less green out here," Dan noted, watching the forest thin out as they grew closer to Scotsdale.

Lucas nodded, knowing what he meant. Greenford looked as though it had been carefully dropped into the middle of a dense forest. Scottsdale was located at the edge of the forest and had been more dedicated to trimming back nature. It didn't hurt that it was located where the forest gave way to grassy plains.

"I swear, whenever I have to travel out of Greenford, even to Scotsdale," Lucas began, turning on his signal to transfer lanes on the road. "It always feels like I'm traveling a lot further than I am. It's always amazed me how Greenford has spread out as far as it has but never quite lost that...I don't know, wild feeling."

"I've always found it peaceful," Dan said, watching the tree line still. "I spend so much of my time in the club, where it's either kinda creepy dark and quiet, or full of so much noise and people you can't think, it's nice to just...walk around and hear the birds, smell the trees, whatever."

"It's something my mother always loved," Lucas said. "I think it's why she wanted to raise us here. Greenford is just big enough to make sure we were exposed to different people, but small enough to feel homey and calm."

Dan chuckled. "It's funny. I came here years ago to go to the University. Ended up getting the job at Nocturne and quit school so I could figure things out. Tried going back but still hadn't figured things out. So now I'm still at Nocturne, still in Greenford and...I don't know if I'll ever figure things out. But I know I want to stay in Greenford."

"You're not that old," Lucas said, glancing at him and finding his eyes sweeping over Dan's body before snapping back to the road. "There's still plenty of time to figure things out."

Dan snorted, taking another drink from the apparently bottomless cup. "That's what people keep telling me. But I can't exactly keep working as a stripper forever. The clock is ticking before I have to have *something*. Otherwise, I'm going to end up flipping burgers or going back to school and burning through more student loan debt than I've already collected."

Lucas considered that carefully. He had never really struggled to know what he was going to do with his life. It had taken a little bit of time to narrow down that he wanted to turn his focus onto criminal law, but he'd always known he wanted to be a lawyer. That had been decided in his sophomore year of high school and had never wavered.

He could imagine how frustrating it had to be, going through life and not being quite sure what you enjoyed. Especially because he knew Dan enjoyed what he already did, but there really was a time limit for that. Stripping wasn't something that could last indefinitely, and eventually, Dan would be left with little more than...

"Why not open or run a club of your own?" Lucas asked.

Dan glanced at him. "What?"

"After all, you've been working in one for quite a few

years now. You clearly have the experience and skill for running one. Otherwise, Mr. Morales wouldn't consistently leave *you* in charge when he went away," Lucas pointed out, nodding to himself as he did so. "Based on what I recall Mat telling me, Nocturne isn't running any differently or less smoothly now with you temporarily in control. As I said before, you have a good head on your shoulders. You clearly aren't struggling with managing people, numbers, or various odds and ends. It's something worth considering if you enjoy what you're doing, you could look at managing and owning a place as an extension of what you're doing now."

Dan had turned in his seat to watch Lucas intently the entire time he was talking. When Lucas was finished, he spared a glance toward the other man and was relieved to see a small smile on his face before Dan turned back toward the window.

"That," Dan began, then nodded. "Is actually not a half-bad idea, Lucas. And again, thank you. It's nice to have things put into perspective...and it's nice to hear good things about yourself."

"They're things I feel you should take into consideration," Lucas told him, looking for their upcoming exit.

"So," Dan said, and Lucas could hear the tone of his voice shift. "Are all those things the reason why you totally tried to kiss me? Or was it just my ass in tiny underwear?"

If Lucas was old enough, he would have sworn the man was trying to give him a heart attack. As it was, he barely managed to stay in his own lane. Though if that was because of what Dan said or because of the imagery it conjured forth in his head, he didn't know.

Dan let out a light laugh as the car swerved, holding onto the door. "I'm guessing it was probably the ass...huh?"

"That," Lucas began, trying to find the words and found

himself scrambling mentally instead. "Is not the world's easiest answer to give."

"Interesting," Dan said, sounding thoughtful. "Is this the universe's way of telling me that my ass is so great I can make straight guys question their sexuality with one little dance?"

"It wasn't the dance," Lucas blurted out.

Dan looked at him, raising a brow. "What?"

"Well, not *just* the dance," Lucas said, wincing as he realized he really was going to commit to the conversation. "The dance...well, anyway. It was before that."

"When?"

"When you offered for me to come out the next night."

"What was so special about that?"

"You were uh...wearing that underwear. That...*little* underwear," Lucas managed to get out, feeling his face grow warm. "It caught my attention."

He knew full well he was stumbling over his words and sounding like a complete idiot in the process. Yet, if that was the case, Dan didn't seem bothered by it in the slightest. In fact, the man was watching Lucas intently, and from the corner of his eye, Lucas could see a delighted smirk on the man's face.

"So yeah," Dan said, settling back into his seat. "It was my ass."

Lucas considered how to respond to that but settled on a quiet, "Yes."

Dan gave a soft noise of thought, watching as the buildings of Scotsdale took up their surroundings. "Is that a problem for you?"

"That's a very good question," Lucas said, liking the conversation a little bit more now that it moved less into the blatantly sexual and more into the core of his issue. "I have never once been attracted to another man in my life."

"So, it's not that your sexuality could be different than you thought?" Dan mused. "Or at least, not in the sense of 'oh gross' or something like that."

Lucas couldn't help his bark of laughter. "If men being with other men was a disgusting thought to me, I'm sure Mat would have known by now. The only time I find it gross is when it's my brother and his fiancé shoving their tongues down each other's throats in full view of anyone who might stumble into a communal room."

"I'd watch it."

"He's not your brother."

"True."

"So no," Lucas continued, not wanting to linger on the traumatizing topic of his brother's sex life in detail. "Same-sex attraction doesn't upset me, bother me, or disgust me. I have no negative feelings associated with gay or bi men."

"That's a very efficient summary. You really covered all your bases there."

"Force of habit."

Dan smirked, watching him as they stopped at a light. "So, what is it?"

"I'm in my thirties," Lucas explained as he rounded the corner once the light turned green. "If there were even the slightest inclination that I could have been into other men, it should have shown itself by now. I'm not a complete recluse, and I've been around a great many different types of people. And yet there hasn't been the slightest hint, not the faintest little twitch."

"So, it's that it's different and doesn't make sense to you," Dan summarized slowly. "Because you feel like it should."

"When you put it like that, I sound unreasonable and ridiculous," Lucas grumbled, keeping an eye out for the location.

Dan chuckled, reaching out to pat Lucas on the shoulder. "A little, but I don't hold it against you. I mean, c'mon, do you really expect it to make sense?"

"Most things do."

"Most things that aren't having to do with people maybe. But people rarely make sense."

"I make sense."

"Really? Then why are you turned on by another guy for the first time in your life?"

Lucas flashed back to Friday afternoon in the office. His hands down his pants and coming because he had been focused on the idea of the other man's bare ass on full display, just for him.

"Or," Dan said, leaning forward to look over Lucas. "There's more than just being turned on going on in that brain of yours."

Lucas should have known the other man would be good at reading expressions. Especially when it came to someone being turned on or not. The man's entire livelihood depended on that knowledge and successfully utilizing it.

"You know," Dan said as they pulled into the parking lot. "There is a way for you to figure out if it's something you need to pay attention to or just something you should ignore."

"What's that?" Lucas asked as he drove toward the spot where he saw a lone car parked.

"Do what the college kids do these days. What you never got around to doing apparently."

"Again, what?"

"Experiment."

"With you?"

"Who else is turning you on without warning?"

Lucas wanted to protest because it should have sounded like an absurd idea. The thing was, his analytical brain grabbed onto the idea and immediately began turning it over, inspecting it carefully. After all, unless something was obviously dangerous to himself or others, he shouldn't outright dismiss it. Sometimes simply trying a theory on for size was often the best way to either confirm its validity or quickly deny it. If he well and truly wanted to know if this was simply a fluke, a one-off, or just the wiring of his brain going crazy for some reason, there really was only one...

"Oh shit," Lucas muttered as the driver's side door of the other car opened.

Dan's brow raised, his attention snapping to watch the woman get out of the car. "Who's that?"

Lucas grimaced. "My ex."

DAN

Dan couldn't help his snicker as he watched the woman stand up straight and stare at the car with a mingled expression of annoyance and impatience. The woman wasn't very tall, perhaps a couple of inches shorter than Dan. Her dark blonde hair fell around the shoulders of her gray suit, and her eyes were only a shade darker than Dan's. His laughter, however, came from when she turned to adjust the side of her skirt, and the curve of her ass, prominent and obvious, was put on display.

"What is so funny?" Lucas asked, sounding grumpy as he checked himself over.

"You just," Dan began, trying to contain his laughter. "Apparently have a type."

"A..." Dan began and looked at the woman again, blanching in sudden realization.

"You're an ass man, got it," Dan said with another laugh, getting out of the car.

"Mr. Masterbaum?" the woman asked politely, flashing him a perfectly professional smile.

He winced, holding out his hand. "Dan, or Daniel,

please. The less I hear my last name, the less I think about the masturbation jokes everyone made in junior high and high school."

She chuckled, shaking his hand. "I can't say I blame you, Dan it is. I'm Kimberly Florret, but Kimberly or Kim is fine by me."

"Kim it is," he said with a grin.

"Good afternoon, Kimberly," Lucas said in a neutral voice as he stepped around the car to greet her.

Dan watched as the woman's face twitched, almost falling into a scowl when Lucas approached. She was apparently still quite aware of Dan's presence, so instead, her smile simply spasmed downward before reasserting itself.

"Lucas," she said smoothly. "I wasn't aware that you were retreating back to your roots."

"I'm not," Lucas said, flashing a smile. "Doing a favor for my brother and Dan."

"How nice of you to take time from your schedule. I know how busy you normally are."

"I take the time when I can."

"So it seems."

The conversation was perfectly normal, sounded even friendly, but Dan could feel the chilly air coming off both of them. Apparently, whatever their relationship had been before, it hadn't ended on a good note or recovered in the meantime.

Rather than stand between them and wonder at how it could feel like the middle of winter with a July sun beating down on them, Dan walked away to inspect the building. It had originally been a small packaging plant but the owners had gone under in the mid-nineties and it had been passed around ever since. Despite just over two and half decades since its last owner, it wasn't in the worst shape.

The windows along the front would either need to be replaced or outright removed. The brick exterior was genuine but crumbling in a few places, but not so terribly that whole chunks of the entire building would have to be removed. He would have to see the inside, but he thought that if the exterior had managed to stave off serious neglect, he had a good feeling about the interior.

Dan turned on his heel to face the two professionals politely pretending to watch him. "You two done?"

"Pardon?" Kimberly asked, blinking innocently at him.

Dan motioned between her and Lucas. "Well, you two were...catching up, so I figured I'd give you a minute or two. Didn't want to interrupt."

Kimberly flashed him a smile while Lucas frowned at him. "No problem. I assumed you would want to check the place out for yourself before we started discussing the details."

Dan beamed at her. "Absolutely. Take me on the grand tour."

She reached into her jacket and pulled out a ring of keys, jingling them. "If you'll follow me."

Kimberly didn't spare a glance at Lucas as she marched toward the double doors that made up the front. Dan waited until Lucas stepped forward, falling in line beside him.

"You two seem like you're great friends," Dan commented idly.

Lucas grimaced. "I believe she would prefer I exist somewhere other than an hour drive from where she lives and works. Had I been thinking, I would have been prepared that she might be the agent who would show us around."

"What, and reschedule until another one showed up?" Dan asked.

Lucas shook his head. "No, I would have just been prepared, was all."

Dan couldn't add much more as they reached Kimberly and she unlocked the doors. She reached in and hit a switch in the cool darkness, lighting up the space. It was a small entry room, covered in dust and cobwebs. Dan could see the area split off into the main room, as well as toward another dark room without a door.

"That," she told him, pointing toward the dark gap in the wall. "Was a former storage room, a little dirty in there but that's true of everything here."

"Could be a good place to set up a checkpoint," Dan mused. "Get cover charges and hang up coats."

She nodded, leading him through the next set of doors and into the expansive room that had been the factory floor. The ceiling was high, and Dan toyed with the idea of recreating the second floor from Nocturne. He could certainly see a sort of VIP area working out in the new club as well as it did in Nocturne, albeit with fewer private dances open to people.

"The machinery was all removed years ago," Kimberly told them, motioning to the large patches of the floor that were lighter in color than the rest of the dirty concrete. "And the wiring was updated a couple of years ago. Of course, anything you would want to add would be purely on your budget."

Dan nodded, then pointed toward the back. "Where do those doors lead?"

She motioned for him to follow. "Come with me. But do me a favor and stay behind me while we walk around."

Dan frowned in confusion, glancing up toward Lucas who gave another grimace. "May I ask why?"

"A few years ago, there was an incident at another factory where some...not so nice people had taken it over. A drug cartel, I'm told. That and we have had a few people take up residence in big abandoned buildings before, and they're not always happy to be found," Kimberly told him.

"Ahh," Dan began nervously as she bent down to unlock the doors. "No offense but you and I combined are like, maybe Lucas's weight. Why are you going first?"

Lucas chuckled, but it was Kimberly who flashed a smile, pulling her jacket back to reveal a holster with a gun tucked neatly inside it. "Because little ol' me has quite a sizable amount of firepower on her."

"You know," Dan said with a chuckle. "If I was even remotely into women, I would be sorely tempted to ask what you're doing after you get off work."

"Aw, you're sweet," she told him, stepping into the dark to shuffle around before the lights came on.

"And *why* do you think I was so attracted to her at first?" Lucas muttered to him.

"Because her gun is bigger than yours?" Dan asked with a wicked grin.

Lucas side-eyed him. "You haven't seen my gun to know."

Dan's eyes widened, a sudden thrill and curiosity jolting through him. Before he could do more than glance down at Lucas's crotch and wonder just what the man was talking about, Kimberly returned. Dan was a little thankful for her polite look of curiosity, interrupting him. He was pretty sure the words that came out of his mouth would have been wondering if big guns ran in the family, and he really didn't want to associate him with Mateo in Lucas's mind.

There were only a few bulbs in the short hallway. There were another set of doorways, one to the left with a closed door and another to the right, big enough for two doors but instead an empty space.

"The locker rooms for the workers were down there," Kimberly told them, pointing to the right. "I don't know if the plumbing still works right in them but I'll be sure to ask."

"Well, places need a bathroom," Dan told her with a shrug. "I'm sure we could retool it into one. Might want to take the showers out though, lord knows what people would get up to in there."

"Following your logic," she said, opening the other door. "We have a back area with a room that was used for all the filing and another room that was used as the office for the on-shift supervisor."

"A cooler and a manager's office," Dan added with a grin.

She flashed him a smile. "I have to admit, when I heard what you wanted to use the location for, I couldn't deny that it would be a good use of the building. It would require some investment, of course, but if the right amount of work was put in..."

"Well, this certainly is shaping up to meet my expectations," Dan said, glancing at Lucas who was peering at one of the walls closely. His thoughts hiccupped for a moment as he watched Lucas lean forward, pushing his ass out to press against the fabric of the man's slacks. Unlike Lucas, Dan wasn't strictly an ass man, but that didn't mean he couldn't appreciate a nice one, even if it was just nice to grab onto.

"Well, it will all depend on *exactly* what kind of establishment you're trying to put here," Kimberly continued, interrupting his thoughts. Which he was grateful for, now that he knew Lucas could potentially want something more out of him than just a professional relationship, Dan was starting to be more distracted by the man's presence.

Dan flashed the woman a smile. "Don't worry, we know. We have no intention of putting in a strip club here. And even if it wasn't against Scotsdale's bylaws, we wouldn't want to open up something that would more or less be competition to our home business either. A club will work just fine for people who want to drink and listen to music but don't want a bunch of men and women getting naked on stage to interrupt it."

Kimberly winked at him. "Their loss. I've seen a couple of your performances, you're quite good."

Dan beamed. "Thank you. I enjoy myself, and it's still a hell of a lot of fun to see other people enjoying it."

"And there are plenty," Lucas muttered, now eyeing what appeared to be a pipe of some sort.

Kimberly glanced at him in open surprise. "You've gone?"

Dan chuckled. "I convinced him to come out and give the place a try for one night. Just to have a little fun."

"And he *went*?"

"That he did. Had himself some drinks, saw the show, had some more drinks, and I'm pretty sure he enjoyed himself."

Lucas turned to look at him, his expression almost unreadable. Dan would have paid good money to know what was flitting through the man's thoughts at that moment. And really, he hoped Lucas was remembering the dance all too clearly.

"Well," Kimberly said, sounding impressed. "Maybe you should hang around Lucas some more. Lord knows he could use someone to poke him out of his cave once in a while and see the world."

"The opinion held by you and so many other people apparently," Lucas muttered.

"I can't imagine why," she said dryly.

"Well," Dan interrupted, not sure if he should let them continue or just be pleased that she thought he was a good influence on Lucas. "I suppose I'll have to get an estimate of what sort of work we'd have to have done."

"I can forward all relevant information to you and Lucas," Kimberly told him, leading them back out into the main room and toward the parking lot. "There's no rush on deciding if you want to buy the place or not. So far, the only people showing any interest are...well, you and your boss."

"That's good to know," Dan chuckled, waiting for her to close and lock the doors to the factory behind them. "I'm sure Rico will be pretty happy when I tell him what I found and think we can work with. But he'll be less happy, I'm sure, when I finally get an idea of what it'll cost to do everything."

Dan remembered what Lucas had told him might be worth considering and the idea lit up in his head. There was certainly an allure to the idea of opening up his own club and running it. He could never afford all the bills on something like this new place, though with his savings and a personal loan, he might be able to scrape together half if his own internal calculations were right. Maybe he could hope his years of credit would be good enough to go for a business loan.

"You still have the same email?" Kimberly asked Lucas.

Lucas nodded. "Same one for the office."

"Alright, and I have yours as well, Dan," she said, looking down at her phone. "I'll have everything to you both by the end of the day. And then...one of you call when you figure out what you're going to do."

"Thank you for taking the time to show us around," Lucas told her, holding his hand out.

She snorted. "Of course. And tell your mom I said hi. I miss that crazy woman sometimes."

"I'll deliver the message," Lucas promised and Dan could see the man meant it. There was barely a defrosting between them but damned if he didn't believe that Lucas would really pass the message along.

Dan was feeling pretty good by the time they got in the car and headed out. Both ideas for the future club and the number-crunching involved to get it going. He suspected he would have to have the place inspected for any hazardous material that would need to be cleaned up and then get someone out to at least pick the place up. The wiring and pipes would have to be checked, and he would need a good idea of the layout of the place and decide where to put things before they really started planning.

"Did it bother you that I kissed you?" Lucas asked.

Dan jerked out of his thoughts, looking around the car. He hadn't realized how deeply he'd been in his head until he saw they were back on the freeway. Obviously, he had been lost in thought and either Lucas had been brooding about the night at Nocturne the entire time, trying to drum up the courage to say something, or it had popped out of his mouth suddenly.

From what he was coming to understand about the other man, it was more likely the former.

"Bother me?" Dan asked, shaking his head. "I was taken off guard. I wasn't expecting it to happen. And that you took off so fast. And for the record, you didn't actually kiss me, you *almost* kissed me and then ran off."

"You certainly do have a way of making me sound so well put together when you describe me."

Dan laughed. "It's what you did, though."

"I know," Lucas said softly, wincing. "It just kind of bubbled up in my head and wouldn't go away."

"Kissing me?"

"Well...sort of. That just came into my head suddenly, and then I was doing it. The next thing I knew, I was backing away and running off."

Dan frowned. "Alright, then you've lost me. What exactly was 'bubbling' away in your head for so long?"

Lucas shifted in his seat, still not having looked over at Dan. He could tell the man was struggling with the thoughts in his head, and Dan's heart went out to him. It undoubtedly couldn't be easy to suddenly have the possibility of your worldview being shifted without warning. Especially when you were someone like Lucas, who had a very steady and consistent worldview.

"The dance," Lucas admitted, shifting again. "And...you know."

Dan was starting to suspect that the man wasn't shifting around out of *physical* discomfort. "Ah, my butt."

"Yes. That."

"So. You were thinking about my ass for a while."

"Yes."

"And that made you want to kiss me."

"That more or less sums up the tale, yes."

Dan nodded in understanding. "So, you were taken aback by the fact that you liked my ass in a nice pair of underwear. And you were a little surprised to find out you *really* liked my ass while I was on stage."

"Again, good summation."

"Does that apply to everything about me?"

"Like, your whole body?"

Dan nodded again. "My body. My personality. The idea of sex in general with me."

Lucas frowned, moving into the right-hand lane to let someone pass in the silence. "Well, I can't say much about the rest of your body. I wasn't really paying attention and I don't really know. As for your personality, I have enjoyed that, certainly. You're a happy person, a bright spot among people, you're lighthearted and you know how to make me feel comfortable even while you're doing your own thing."

Dan didn't bother to hide his pleasure at that. "And the rest?"

"I don't know."

"Did you consider what I said earlier?"

"The experimentation bit?"

"That's the one."

Lucas sighed, then shrugged. "I can't say I've thought about it a whole lot. There hasn't been time to think too heavily on it since we talked."

Dan was beginning to suspect that Lucas thinking too heavily about it was precisely the problem. "So, that's not you saying no."

"I cannot see a flaw in the reasoning so far, no," Lucas admitted.

Dan grinned, seeing the upcoming sign. "Could you pull off at the rest stop?"

Lucas frowned at him in confusion. "Are you alright?"

Dan smirked as Lucas was already pulling off into the small driveway toward the thankfully empty rest stop. "Yeah, just pull around to the back, away from the highway."

"Uh," Lucas began, realization trickling into his voice. "Dan?"

"Feel free to drive on by if you don't like the idea that just entered your head," Dan told him, meaning it though suspecting the offer wasn't taken.

He wasn't surprised to find that instead, Lucas pulled into a parking spot under the shade of a tall tree.

LUCAS

His heart pounded as he pulled into the shaded parking spot. Lucas knew damn well that Dan wasn't asking him to pull over just to talk to him or because he needed to use the bathroom. The other man was practically leering at him from the passenger seat and it didn't take much thinking for Lucas to know what the man had on his mind.

And yet there he was, pulling over, allowing it to happen.

Lucas hesitated a moment before turning the car off and sitting still, staring out the front window. Dan wasn't looking at him, but Lucas could feel the man's attention locked on him, waiting.

"Dan," Lucas managed, still unsure what he wanted to say.

Dan looked at him, and though Lucas didn't meet his eyes, he could see the man smiling. "I'm going to do one thing and one thing only. If you want it to stop before, during, or right after, you let me know immediately, got it?"

"Dan..."

"Which means now is also a chance to say no."

Lucas said nothing, nodding his understanding.

"If it stops or goes on to something else, it's for you to tell me no. You say the word and everything stops, and I never bring up anything again. You get to live your life exactly how you did before, no questions asked."

Lucas couldn't help but smile faintly at that one. "Is this a negotiation?"

"This is me putting my foot on the gas but giving you control of the brakes."

"I...okay."

"Good, now I need you to look at me."

Lucas did, swallowing hard when he caught Dan's gaze peering up at him. He suddenly realized at that moment just how much smaller than him Dan really was. Lucas had never given much thought to the man's size, despite his having to constantly look down at Dan. Maybe it was just Dan's sheer confidence or the pure size of his personality, but he had never struck Lucas as being smaller than him before.

Dan shifted closer to him, and Lucas realized what he was going to do. He couldn't bring himself to move, but neither did he try to reach out and stop Dan either. Warm fingers, soft, and strong, curled around the back of his neck, holding onto him. Lucas's breath caught in his throat, and then Dan's lips were on his.

At first, there was nothing, just the flash of shock at the expected kiss and a dull curiosity at the change in sensation from what he was used to. It wasn't totally different from a chaste kiss with a woman, although Lucas could feel the man's stubble brushing against his. There was less softness to the cheeks that brushed his own and the fingers at his neck.

When Dan's mouth stirred, Lucas snapped out of the

disconnected haze, going taut when the tip of a tongue slid over his bottom lip. A switch flipped in his mind somewhere, lighting the dark corners and banishing the shadows of doubt as he reached out and took hold of Dan, pulling him closer.

As their lips parted, tongues making tentative and then bolder moves to taste the other, Lucas found he didn't really care all that much that Dan was a man. The slight but rough brush of stubble against his face was new but strangely enticing, no different than skin brushing skin in his suddenly heated mind. The hand on his neck squeezed tight, holding him there and demanding, but still allowing Lucas to move if he so wanted.

Which, Lucas *was* moving, but it was toward the other man rather than trying to get away. Dan struggled to find a position to sit comfortably, his hand coming down to rest on Lucas's thigh as he tried to keep himself upright. Whether through intention or sheer dumb luck, it happened to come to rest on Lucas's straining cock.

Pleasure rippled through Lucas, forcing a sharp gasp of air. For a moment, he considered what he wanted the other man to do, his thoughts bouncing from the sudden surge of desire Dan had caused in him and the natural wariness that made him wonder if they were going at too high a speed.

Once more, Dan decided to push toward the next step, his fingers sliding up the length of Lucas's cock as it was pressed against his thigh. Lucas shivered as the man's fingers reached the button of his pants, hesitated, then flipped them open, pulling down the zipper effortlessly.

"Remind me," Dan muttered against his lips as his fingers slipped down into Lucas's underwear and wrapped around his cock. "To never doubt your 'gun' again."

"No puns," Lucas groaned, though that was mainly due to Dan's hands pulling him free and stroking.

"Yes, sir," Dan said, voice low and teasing.

Lucas kissed him again, pulling Dan closer as the man began to pump, his movements stopping long enough to run a gentle thumb over the leaking head. Any doubt Lucas might have had about what they were doing quickly evaporated as he focused on the feel of Dan's hand, the press of his body against his, and the taste of him on his tongue.

Dan was certainly no stranger to what he was doing. Whether that was from practicing on himself or on other people, Lucas neither knew nor cared. Dan moved his hand carefully at first, testing to see what worked and what didn't, all while keeping the kiss going and Lucas distracted from thinking too heavily. Lucas knew he was in trouble when Dan found just the right grip and began slowly sliding his hand up, letting his palm slide along the underside of the sensitive head.

There was plenty of friction, enough to send chills and shivers through Lucas as he gave himself to the other man's ministrations. There was no lube on hand to make sure there wasn't *too* much friction, but Dan was careful as he worked Lucas's cock. Once more, Lucas found himself realizing it had been a few days since he'd taken care of himself. Since the incident in his office, in fact.

The thought was enough to make him jerk in Dan's hand. Without thinking, he let his hand slide down, cupping Dan's ass as the man practically bowed over him to keep going. It was soft in his hand, but there was enough muscle from whatever workouts Dan did to provide a pleasing firmness as his fingers sank in. To his surprise, Dan moaned against his lips, fingers tightening their grip.

Those two things were enough for Lucas, and though he

was mindful that there could be *someone* around to hear him, he couldn't stifle his groan completely. Dan kissed him harder as Lucas's cock twitched, cum pouring out over his fingers and splattering against the steering wheel. Lucas gasped as the last wave of pleasure shuddered through him, leaving him lightheaded.

It took several seconds before he realized there was a mess to clean up. Dan was watching him from the passenger seat with amusement as Lucas pulled wipes out from the center console and handed an opened one to Dan. With another, Lucas cleaned up the wheel and the few spots that had landed on his slacks. He might get away with no one noticing them since most of it had landed on Dan.

"So," Lucas said, giving one last wipe of the wheel. "That was...something."

"This is the part where I would ask you how you feel," Dan said, voice warm and a little amused. "But I have a very strong suspicion that you really wouldn't know how to answer that question at the moment."

Lucas glanced at him, smiling softly. "You have a very good assessment of my character, it seems."

Dan winked. "So, I'm not going to ask. I'll let you think on things like you need to."

"Just like you let me think about this?" Lucas asked, motioning to his crotch and realizing he hadn't tucked himself away. "Damn."

Dan chuckled as Lucas readjusted himself. "Don't put it away on my account."

Lucas rolled his eyes. "I was distracted."

Dan smiled again, leaning over to surprise Lucas with a light kiss on the cheek. "Look, I didn't give you time to think too hard on things this time because...people sometimes should do stuff they want, when they want, even if they're worried about doing it. Not *everything* has to be thought about. But..."

"But?" Lucas asked, genuinely curious at the man's thought process.

"But there's a difference between overthinking something you want to do and needing to think over something you've already done," Dan explained with a shrug.

Lucas gave him a crooked grin. "And I wanted to do that?"

Dan glanced at him, a slight sharpness to his gaze. "I thought so, but that's why I gave you the choice to say no at any time."

Lucas hesitated and then realized what he'd all but come right out and say. "I'm sorry. I wasn't trying to...infer that you pushed the boundaries or went too far without consulting me."

The sharpness disappeared, the mistake forgiven instantly. "I know, or I hoped that's what you meant. But just in case, I didn't, right?"

Lucas shook his head. "No. I may not know what I'm thinking or feeling at the moment, but that doesn't make you the bad guy in any way. Like you said, I was in control of the brakes, and I never pressed down."

"I guess you didn't," Dan said with a smile that made Lucas's gaze linger on his face a moment longer.

"So, now what?" Lucas asked, suddenly unsure.

Dan flopped back in his seat, chuckling. "Now, you go back to your office, I go into my temporary office, and we go on with our adult responsibilities. You give it some thought and come to your own conclusions. If you wanna share those with me, you have my number, you know where I work, and if you want, I can tell you where I live."

"Life as normal then," Lucas said turning on the car.

"Life as normal," Dan reaffirmed as they pulled out of the parking lot.

"YOU KNOW," Samuel said, leaning forward onto the table between them to peer at Lucas. "Not that I'm not used to you being quiet on occasion, but you've been...*abnormally* quiet tonight."

Lucas frowned down at the pasta dish in front of him. Somehow the meal wasn't as good as usual. Which was strange, as the little Italian place he and Samuel liked to frequent had always had good quality food before. It had been the first place he and Samuel had eaten at, back when they were strangers but meeting for a professional networking arrangement. Samuel taught law at the university, and his opinions and connection to the educational side of the law would have come in handy for someone actively practicing law.

Of course, Lucas hadn't known at the time that he would find in Samuel a kindred spirit, one who could be as dry and sarcastic as him, all while maintaining a good sense of humor in general. They were both analytical, often to the point of being accused of overthinking. And yes, Samuel had made the fantastic point that once upon a time, Lucas had encouraged his friend not to stay safe in his little bubble of the world and be willing to expand out to greater, different experiences.

"I am not," Lucas finally said, eyeing a piece of shrimp. "And I think they overcooked my food."

"You're right about the second thing, I'll give you that much."

"Seriously."

"Mona already warned us that the main chef was out sick."

Lucas looked up, unthinkingly looking for the woman who had worked as a server at the restaurant and not finding her. "Oh. I suppose I wasn't listening."

"So I gathered," Samuel said dryly, taking a sip of his wine. "If you weren't feeling sociable, you didn't have to agree to come out and eat. You could have waited until Caleb and I had our little get-together."

Lucas shook his head. "No, no. I'm sorry. I've got a lot on my plate at the moment, and my head is everywhere but in the present. The whole point of coming out was to enjoy myself a little and do it sober."

"Do it sober?" Samuel asked with a raised brow. "Did I miss something? Did you get smashed at another holiday party...in the middle of summer?"

Lucas groaned. "I really wish you wouldn't feel the need to bring that up."

Samuel snickered. "I invited my best friend to a faculty Christmas party. Where he promptly had way too much of the punch and proceeded to act like a horny frat boy."

"I was not *that* bad," Lucas protested, though it didn't feel that far from the truth.

Whoever had made the punch deserved a swift kick in the ass for not warning how ridiculously strong they had made it and still somehow managed to conceal the taste for the most part. And yes, maybe he had forgotten how to moderate his volume, and yes, maybe he had tried to flirt with a few of the female faculty members. Thankfully, they had found it amusing rather than insulting or harassing, but Lucas still did not like to recall that night.

Or the morning after, for that matter.

"You were pretty bad," Samuel countered with a chuckle. "But at least you didn't try to do a keg stand."

"There was no keg."

"It's the thought that counts."

Lucas rolled his eyes. "You're never going to let me live that down, are you?"

"Oh God, not on your life. So long as I have that memory in my head, it's going to be in yours as well."

"I can only pray for early-onset dementia then."

Samuel was looking smug again and Lucas knew his friend had purposefully brought up that abysmal memory to get a rise out of him. That it had worked only made it all the worse. And that he'd probably needed to be dragged out of his constant overthinking was completely and utterly beside the point.

It had been a few days since he'd last seen Dan. They had met up the day after going out to the building to inspect it, but neither of them had brought up what had happened in the car. Lucas had left the club unsure whether what he felt was relief or disappointment, and that alone required a good few hours of internal debate to make up his mind.

He still wasn't sure, though he suspected it had been both.

"Do you think sexualities can change far later than one's teens or early twenties?" Lucas asked as he reached for his own wine glass.

Samuel froze, looking up slowly to blink owlishly at Lucas. "Uh, that's quite the loaded question you've just dropped in my lap, Lucas. Got uh, something on your mind?"

"Clearly I have the question I just asked on my mind," Lucas pointed out dryly.

"You know, I'm flattered and all," Samuel said slowly,

though the small hints of a smirk on the man's face ruined anything serious he might have been trying to feign.

Lucas picked a piece of shrimp off his plate and chucked it at Samuel. "I have *some* standards, thank you very much."

"Are you trying to say my boyfriend has low standards?"

"I'm saying that he should probably be checked out by a medical professional. Or at least a psychiatric one."

Samuel shrugged. "I've been telling him that for years. But noooo, he says it's love."

"And you sit there and pretend like that doesn't make you all warm and gooey inside whenever he says it," Lucas said as he popped pasta into his mouth.

"Maybe," Samuel said with a smirk.

"Now, answer my question."

Samuel sighed. "Are you going to give me the reason why you suddenly decided to talk about sexuality when you've literally never brought it up before?"

"No."

"Fine, but that just tells me this isn't an idle question," Samuel said, taking a slow drink. "And I don't know. Sexuality is weird, I mean, *people* are weird, so why shouldn't something like sex be weird in their heads? I mean, there are guys who discover they're gay or bi after a divorce or whatever."

"Or they were the whole time," Lucas pointed out.

"That's kinda sorta my point," Samuel shrugged, pushing his plate away. "We like to think we know all about ourselves, like what we see is what we get. But we don't, not really. It gets easy to ignore little things or outright bury them, and we never realize what else we're holing up in the process. Just look at how I was. If it wasn't for Caleb coming back into my life and being a good guy for me, making me realize I had to work on myself, I wouldn't have bothered going to therapy."

"It did seem to do you a lot of good," Lucas noted, setting his glass aside.

"It did. But I'm not saying that everyone needs to go running to therapy when they figure out something might be different or off about them."

"And what would you say they should do?"

"I don't know, find out if they're discovering something new for the fun time or the long time."

Lucas already knew Samuel was suspicious about his reasons for asking, so he thought it safe to take Samuel's advice as the direct sort. He thought it amusing that Samuel, of all people, was advocating risk and branching out into new ground. Then again, it was exactly the sort of thing Lucas himself had encouraged his friend to do, and he was happy to say that it seemed to have done Samuel a great deal of good.

Samuel leaned forward and flashed him a smile. "Look. If this is you...questioning yourself, whether you have a reason or not."

"Covering your bases, I note," Lucas said with a chuckle.

Samuel grinned. "Then don't fret about it too much, alright? Maybe consider it the same way I had to consider Caleb coming back into my life, a wake-up call. Maybe you've been doing the same thing for so long that you've somehow tricked yourself into being open to new things."

"So, possibly being into another guy is because I'm bored?" Lucas asked with a raised brow.

Samuel chuckled, taking Lucas's glass from him and drinking the rest. "No, I'm saying that maybe it's your roundabout way of figuring out more about yourself. And thank you for finally confirming that there is, in fact, a guy who's making you question what dick tastes like."

"I regret everything, including this friendship," Lucas groaned, shaking his head. "And I hate you."

"Yeah, love you too."

DAN

"And this is the predicted expenses," Dan said, leaning over the desk to hand Rico the sheet of paper in his hand.

Rico looked up from the collection of notes and receipts sitting in front of him on the desk, squinting. Dan knew Rico didn't look it, but the man was pushing past his mid-forties. And while he had no attraction whatsoever to his boss, he sincerely hoped that when he made it to middle-age, he managed to keep himself in as good a shape as Rico did. For how much the man drank, he somehow had stayed away from a massive beer belly.

Rico's thick brow dropped into a heavy frown. "Estimate?"

"Well, it's going to need to be checked for toxic...anything really that might need to be removed. There's the cleaning cost, checking the electrical, pipes, structural integrity..."

Rico waved him off, stopping him before he could continue. "And you're sure this is what I'll be paying?"

Dan shrugged helplessly, he knew how much he had

put down. "Right around that. Truth is, I think I might be a little under what might actually come up, I don't know."

"Christ," Rico muttered, wiping at his mouth. "That's...shit...prices sure have gone up, haven't they?"

Dan winced. "Is this the part where I point out that we're not even including buying the property, going through the fee list for the paperwork, or the lawyer fees?"

Rico eyed him. "Fuck, I hadn't thought of that. What *is* that guy charging anyway?"

Dan opened his mouth and froze when he realized what was about to come out of his mouth.

Rico's brow quirked. "Danny?"

Dan winced heavily, hunching his shoulders as he did so. "I might have...sort have...well, I forgot."

"Forgot what?"

"Forgot to...ask what he was charging before I agreed to have him help us."

Rico scowled at him. "You forgot to ask what the guy was charging? Seriously Dan?"

"I wasn't thinking," Dan protested in a hurry. "You wanted someone quickly and I was getting desperate after the last guy bailed on us. Then Mateo said he'd ask his brother and it never occurred to me to ask what he was charging. I mean, c'mon, Mateo wouldn't ask his brother if he thought Lucas was going to bankrupt us in the process."

Rico snorted, eyeing the page again. "Yeah, alright, you got me there. Wait, Mateo's brother?"

"Yeah, older brother by a couple of years, I think."

"That's the one I talked to on the phone. Kinda stiff."

Dan chuckled. "A little, at first."

Rico eyed him suspiciously. "Dan, I better not find out you didn't ask this guy his rate because you were too busy checking him out."

"He's straight!" Dan protested.

Though whether that was strictly true was still up for debate. Dan knew full well that curious was curious, and it didn't alter a straight man's sexuality in the slightest. They could enjoy themselves having a bit of fun and move on with their heterosexual lives without ever looking back. He'd been party to it a couple of times and had always kept his distance emotionally from a curiosity-driven partner.

Whether it was a genuine, if new interest, on Lucas's part or just evanescent curiosity that had been sated was yet to be discovered.

"And when has that ever stopped someone from looking?"

"Okay, fine, I looked. But no ass is worth getting *that* distracted over."

"I guess that explains why he got even stiffer when I asked if you'd hit on him."

Dan blinked, taken aback. "What?"

Rico shrugged. "You're a flirter. It's what you do."

"Way to make me sound like a cheap slut, Rico," Dan frowned.

Rico looked up, cocking his head. "A...what? Dan, I run a strip club, where I know damn well y'all aren't just dancing in those private rooms. Would I really give a shit if you're a slut or not? Christ."

Dan snorted. "Fine, but I'm not cheap. That's just rude."

Rico shook his head. "It's nice to know you have your priorities in line."

"So," Dan said, nodding toward the page. "How bad is that?"

"Bad enough to make me want a drink," Rico muttered

as if that was something new. "But not so bad as to make me back out. How've sales been?"

"They're great," Dan shrugged. "Have been forever, you know that."

"Nah," Rico said. "I meant, how's your income been? Ya know I don't keep track of your tips. Bar makes enough on everything else. I don't need to give a shit what gets stuffed into your thong."

Dan grinned, adoring the older man as he had after the first month of working at Nocturne. Rico had always made a show of being grumpy and uncaring and not exactly the most tactful of people. Yet, Dan couldn't imagine working for anyone else. When you scratched the surface, Rico genuinely cared for his employees. He might bitch and moan while he's helping or act like a complete ass, but there were very few people at Nocturne who bought it.

"My sales have been fine," Dan chuckled. "They're going to start dwindling eventually."

"Yeah," Rico agreed, and the sheer ease of it comforted Dan. He didn't need someone to lie and tell him it was going to be alright. It almost reminded him how Lucas had done the same but had provided an alternative option for him to consider.

"I've got a...really nice nest egg I'm sitting on," Dan admitted, thinking about his savings account. "I'm not going to go broke anytime soon but, I've definitely gotta get to thinking about the future."

Rico looked up from the paper once more, watching Dan intensely. "Yeah, I'm sure you do."

"Oh God," Dan groaned. "That's the tone of voice you use when you've had some god-awful idea."

"It is a pretty shit idea," Rico admitted. "But I'm going to stew on it."

"You stew on it," Dan told him with a shake of his head. "But I have a dance to get ready for in a couple of hours. Those Friday night patrons aren't going to be happy if I'm not out there shaking my ass for them."

"To really shit music too," Rico grumbled, setting the paper aside with a thoughtful look.

"I'll be sure to take your criticism into consideration and give substantial thought to changing my dance music repertoire."

"No, you won't."

"No, I won't."

DAN TAPPED on the edge of the mirror as he checked out his reflection. He did his best to consider what would usually work when it came to his performances. It wasn't just that he wanted to put on a good show, though that was part of it, really. He just hated the idea of doing the same shtick for weeks on end, especially after working at Nocturne for years.

"Uh, at the risk of being an idiot," Aidan said from behind him. "What exactly are you going for with this one?"

"You don't sound like an idiot," Dan told him, flashing a smile at him through the reflection of the mirror. "And I have not the slightest idea what to call it. I just liked it when I threw it together."

The undershirt was light and gauzy, a lacy long-sleeve he'd found at a thrift store a few months back. The jeans were black, tight, and ripped up and down the length of the legs, practically shredded. Whoever had owned them before had thrown in some safety pins in different colors and added a few frayed, colorful patches to the bigger holes.

It was all brought together by the long cardigan he'd found online, though instead of thick wool or comfortable cotton, the thing was made out of black fishnet.

Once he'd seen how well the outfit went together, he'd had some fun with the odds and ends lying around the dressing room. Digging through bins of assorted materials and accessories, he'd dug out the fake piercings that he'd used on his brow, his ear, and even one for his lip. He'd thrown on a heavier amount of eyeliner than usual, messed up his hair, and took in the sight.

"I don't know, goth chic? Hipster gone wrong? Kinky but coy?" Dan tried, then wrinkled his nose. "Oh, who cares what's it called. They'll see some little guy dressed up like they're going to a vampire's castle for BDSM night and eat it up."

"Maybe that's what you should have called it," Aidan suggested with a snicker.

"A shame I'm a shit DJ. Otherwise, I might have found a song that probably fit better," Dan said with a laugh. "How you doing over there?"

Aidan, who had gone with a classic go-go boy look, glanced at him and smiled. "I'm alright. It's not that bad, promise."

"I've noticed you do pretty well," Dan told him, meaning it.

For how meek and mild Aidan came off, the young man positively glowed when he was on the stage. Dan had always told Rico that people just had presence, or they didn't. There were plenty of people who looked good in the world, but there were only a select few of those who could pull it off on stage and come off as sexy. Mateo had oozed confidence and masculinity, Dan knew the audience ate up his playfulness and teasing, but Aidan...well, Dan wasn't quite sure how to put words to the man's performance just yet. There was definitely a sexuality there, yet he also felt that it needed more coaxing before it fully shone.

Glam appeared in the dressing room doorway. "Hey, Rico's bitching. It's your time to get out there and get them worked up."

Dan snorted. "Rico, bitching? Never."

Glam rolled his eyes. "Get that little ass out there and make all of us some money, would you?"

"Oh, Glam, you know just how to make a boy feel special and wanted," Dan told him, throwing a spare thong at him.

Glam caught it, looking down at Aidan. As Dan slipped out into the entryway that led to the stage, he caught sight of the bigger man crouching down to talk to Aidan. He had no idea what they had to talk about, but Dan wasn't surprised. Just as much as grumpy Rico cared intensely about the workers, so did stoic Glam. And there really was something endearing about the younger man.

But then the music was starting. Dan closed his eyes, felt the thumping of the beat through his feet. He breathed deeply, letting the thrum of the music sink into his soul, and stepped out onto the stage.

It was exactly as it always was when he stepped out in front of the audience. For a moment, it was impossible to distinguish facial features, giving him only the view of a sea of faceless people all huddled around the edges of the stage. Anxiety rose up, wrapped around a thrill, the moment the roller coaster crests the first hill. And when he posed, inviting the crowd as well as welcoming them, the coaster went over the peak and sped toward the bottom.

He rarely remembered dances in their entirety. His body moved of its own accord and he gave himself to the beat and the excitement of the crowd. He twisted and bent for them, catching a look here and there that he could distinguish among the crowd and feed upon. Pleasure, purely emotional and rooted in his thoughts, pinged and zinged through him as he made a show of himself on the stage.

It wasn't until halfway through the show that he gave a look toward the upper balcony. People rarely stood up there, though there was the occasional loner type or people who wanted a bird's eye view that snuck up there for a show. There were a few at the tables he couldn't see, but right there, almost exactly center stage and gazing down was a face he recognized.

Dan grinned widely, tilting his head back and giving a cheeky wave to Lucas. To his credit, Lucas didn't look ashamed or bashful in the slightest. The man raised his glass in a silent salute, eyes locked on Dan.

After that, it was far more difficult to keep himself in the rhythm of the dance. He had no idea what Lucas was doing back since the man apparently didn't like going out and partying all that much. Dan knew what he *wanted* Lucas to be there for but quietly reminded himself to keep his focus and not let his mind wander. Because he knew full well his idiot head would lead him down a line of thoughts that he didn't need to be having about a confused, if earnest, straight man.

That didn't stop him from making sure to make a display of what he knew was Lucas's favorite asset. The jeans had been a little too dark to really show it off, but the brilliant green, skintight trunks he wore more than made up for it. He made sure not to pay too much attention to the balcony, but he could imagine Lucas's eyes trailing his ass, perhaps even wondering what he might do if that ass was in his grasp.

By the time Dan made his way off stage with another wave, he was glad the music had finally stopped. Though his thoughts had trailed off, they hadn't gone into dangerous territory. Still, his thoughts definitely would have made his show a lot more interesting. Not that he wasn't used to occasionally getting hard during a dance, a product of the environment and thriving on the attention, it was never *totally* hard.

"Good luck," he told Aidan with a wink, making his way toward the back of the dressing room and the small door that housed the shower.

By the time he emerged from the shower and got dressed, he could hear Aidan's set of songs beginning to wind down. He wished he could have watched the man, curious and wanting to peg what it was about the younger man. There would be other nights, though, and he pulled on a pair of dark jeans and a shirt, desperate to get out onto the main floor while the show was still going on.

The next dancer stepped out just as Dan reached the main room. Donna watched him go, raising a brow but saying nothing as she dipped beneath the bar. She emerged a second later with a drink in her hand, silently sliding it to him. Dan gave her a wink and made his way toward the back stairs to go up to the balcony.

When he reached the second floor, he found Lucas standing by the door to the VIP room rather than the balcony's edge. His eyes were on the stage, watching as 'Diamond' twirled and whirled around. Dan had to admit there was a grace to her that no male performer and few female performers managed to pull off. It made up for the slight deficit of stage presence, but she was certainly not lacking admirers.

"Want me to arrange a meet-up?" Dan asked curiously once he was close enough to be heard over the music.

Lucas jerked, almost spilling his drink. "Jesus. I didn't even see you coming."

Dan put his hand atop his head, grinning. "I'm very small. Makes me very sneaky and hard to spot."

Lucas laughed. "I suppose there have to be advantages to being small."

"Well, it makes it easy for a guy to manhandle me too," Dan told him. "Which I have to admit, is really handy."

"I bet," Lucas said in a strange voice.

"So?" Dan asked, glancing at the stage. "Are you interested?"

Lucas's brow furrowed. "Well…"

"In her," Dan specified with a laugh.

Lucas's eyes widened. "Oh. No, that…"

Dan cocked his head as he realized what had just transpired. "Or are you looking to have a meet-up with someone else who works here?"

Lucas fingered the edge of his glass, looking both nervous and determined as he watched Dan's face intently. "I might just."

"Might?" Dan asked, slipping closer. "Or definitely?"

They were close enough that Dan could hear the rough edge to Lucas's voice. "Okay, definitely."

Dan peered up at him, smirking. "So, I'm still technically on the clock…"

"I imagine you would be. Doing another dance?" Lucas asked, still watching Dan carefully.

"Not tonight," Dan said, getting close enough that he could feel Lucas's chest brush against him when the man breathed in deep. "But, if some people were wanting, say...a private dance, I would be on the clock for such a thing."

Lucas swallowed hard, with Dan watching his Adam's apple bob. "A private dance. I..."

Dan eased back half an inch, sensing Lucas's discomfort and not wanting to crowd him. "Of course, if he *doesn't* want that, then I know brakes being tapped when I see them."

Something that Dan thought was panic flashed through Lucas's eyes. Dan had only a moment of confusion before Lucas reached out and took him by the elbow. It was a rough grab, but Dan smiled at it all the same.

"You..." Lucas began, sounding strangled.

"Me?"

"Are the boldest person, I swear to God."

Dan laughed. "That sounds more like a compliment than a criticism."

"That's because it is."

"I'm glad you approve."

"So, a dance?"

"A dance."

"Brakes anytime?"

"At any point whatsoever, no complaints or questions on my part."

Lucas stared at him, and Dan couldn't figure out what he was seeing. The man was apparently not only a heavy thinker but a rapid thinker. Thoughts and emotions flit across the man's face with a speed that was not only unreadable but confusing as hell to try to even glimpse, let alone understand.

"Yeah," Lucas said, nodding woodenly. "Okay."

"Okay?" Dan asked.

"Okay."

"Then let's get somewhere a little more private," Dan said, taking Lucas by the hand and leading him into the VIP room.

LUCAS

As he was led away, Lucas had enough time to wonder if the tension building in him was anxiety or excitement. He then spared a thought that probably, once again, it was both, and he wasn't going to be able to separate those feelings anytime soon. And as they reached the small hallway at the back of the VIP room, he realized he was getting into the habit of being led around by Dan.

And he couldn't see a problem with that.

Dan led him into one of the doorways. The room was a surprise, far less gaudy than he expected it to be. The floor looked like wood, a small beige rug under a black loveseat that sat at the back. An office chair, straight-backed and plush, sat beside one wall where a cabinet full of different decanters and bottles sat.

"It looks like an office," Lucas realized.

Dan laughed, turning to face him. "I thought maybe something a little less...flashy would probably feel better for you. This room was actually my idea years ago."

"Why an office?"

"How many people get off on the idea of getting a bit of

fun in the office?"

"Uh...probably many."

"Who aren't you."

Lucas couldn't help but laugh at the observation, nodding. "I have to admit, it's not really been a fantasy of mine. Although..."

"Although?"

He was almost completely sure he wouldn't have said no if Dan had wanted to do this *at* his office instead of a room that looked like one. Which, immediately afterward, he realized he didn't think he could have said no to Dan if the man had asked him to do this anywhere else at all, really. The pounding of his heart might have been nerves, but it was excitement and eagerness as well. Even if it was a little weird to crave, he did crave it, and he felt like there was no way he could back out now, even if he wanted to.

And he really didn't want to.

"Or," Dan said slowly, watching him with a small smile. "We can talk about what your fantasies are at some point."

"At some point?" Lucas asked as he was led to the center of the room.

"First," Dan motioned between the couch and the chair. "Pick where you're going to sit. And then tell me what kind of music you like. I'm sure I can work with just about anything."

"Polka," Lucas told him as he sat down on the couch and watched Dan.

Dan screwed up his features and stared down at the other man. "Your delivery is way too dry. Are you fucking with me or are you serious?" He turned toward a device in the nearby wall. "I don't even know if we have polka on this."

"Are you saying you can't make polka sexy?" Lucas

asked innocently.

Dan turned, peering at the device and cycling through it while Lucas watched him. That it required Dan to bend over and push his ass out in the process was a bonus.

"I can make anything sexy, damn it," Dan grumbled.

Lucas chuckled. "I hate polka."

"Oh, thank God," Dan sighed. "I was so hoping I wasn't going to end up getting sexy to the sound of an accordion."

As much as he appreciated how forward and absolutely positive Dan was, Lucas thought there was plenty endearing about seeing Dan flustered as well. It had only been a moment, but it was enough to make him smile.

"I think they call it Classic Rock now," Lucas said, sounding only mildly offended.

"Classic? Like, big hair rock?"

"Eighties rock."

"Yeah, big hair rock. Metallica, AC/DC, Bon Jovi..."

"If you play 'You Give Love a Bad Name' I'm going to leave," Lucas warned him.

"Oh, pfft," Dan waved him off. "Please. I have something *so* much more cliche than that on this playlist, don't you worry about that."

Lucas cocked his head as the music began and raised a brow. "You're going to give a private dance to...Thunderstruck?"

Dan turned to him, cocking his hips slightly as he smirked. "Trust me, I can manage it. And before you ask, no, this is not the cliché song."

"I'll be sure to keep an ear out," Lucas said, getting comfortable on the couch.

Dan grew closer, leaning over to rest his hands on Lucas's knees. They were close enough that Dan would have only had to lean in a couple of inches to kiss him.

"I'll have to keep in mind that humor makes you less nervous," Dan told him, eyes sweeping up and down Lucas's body.

He had a moment to consider the validity of that statement, but not much longer as Dan finally decided to move. Lucas watched intently as Dan managed to roll his hips, turn and twist his body both gracefully and sensually, and all in a way that he couldn't help but unconsciously notice worked in perfect tandem to the music.

"So," Dan said, voice low but perfectly audible over the music. "I seem to recall that you had a certain...preference for a part of me."

Lucas swallowed, eyes darting around as Dan continued to sway and move, growing closer. "Yes..."

"I do believe," Dan said and Lucas watched in amazement as Dan's pants began to slide down. "It was my ass."

Lucas hadn't spotted the man undoing the buttons to his jeans, but any curiosity over that particular magic trick was gone, much as he was sure Dan was hoping. Lucas honestly had no idea how to refer to the fabric of the underwear Dan was wearing, other than some sort of mesh. It was spaced apart enough to show little flashes of skin as the bright red fabric parted with each movement of Dan's hips, but close enough that it was a tease and little else.

Dan took his time turning around, making sure to flash Lucas a knowing smile as he finally put his ass on display. Lucas watched, breath catching in his throat as the man continued to move with effortless grace. Although Dan had said it to tease him, even Lucas had to admit he was a great fan of a good butt. Dan most certainly had one, and Lucas knew if that ass had been on a woman, he would have been immediately interested. Well, he would have said that originally because as he watched the red fabric-covered globes of

Dan's ass swivel and pivot before him, he had to admit that it didn't really matter at the moment that it was a man attached to the ass.

Lucas knew on some level that there would be a point when Dan would place himself in Lucas's lap, yet he wasn't ready for it when it happened. Despite having to dip, Dan managed to drop with ease, sliding his covered ass in between Lucas's thighs and up the bulge his straining cock was leaving in his pants. A ripple of pleasure went through him, and he couldn't restrain the soft moan of pleasure.

Dan came closer, pressing his back to Lucas's front and wrapping his arms behind him and around Lucas's neck. His ass never stopped moving, sliding up and down Lucas's lap with fluid movements. It was all too easy to picture the man doing the same, but with far fewer clothes and Lucas's cock nestled deep inside him.

"Sweet Jesus," Lucas muttered as the idea centered itself in his thoughts.

"I felt that," Dan chuckled, grinding his ass down firmer. "Just what are you thinking about?"

Lucas knew what answer the man wanted and gave it easily. "Your ass."

Dan's hand fell onto Lucas's, drawing it up and laying it on Dan's thigh. Without missing a beat, Lucas gripped, feeling the muscles twitch and bend as Dan continued the achingly slow grind against his crotch. It was all he needed to bring his hand further up, running it over the man's waist and then beneath the shirt he had kept on instead of his pants.

His heart thundered in his chest, running his hand over the man's stomach, feeling it pulse and thump almost as if to the beat of the music. Lucas gripped it, pulling it up and over Dan's head to toss it away. Warmth flooded his chest as

Dan's heated, bare back fell against him. He never stopped his exploration, finding Dan's body as smooth as his previous partners, but flatter, harder, and all the more fascinating for it.

When Dan turned, it was with a smooth motion that had his knees resting on the couch, a knee on either side of Lucas's hips. He wasn't getting the full view of the man's ass anymore, but he was certainly getting *something*. The smooth planes of Dan's body were on full display as Dan continued to tease, smiling that knowing smile as he did so.

This time, Lucas didn't need the help of moving his hands. He drew them down Dan's back and down the curve of Dan's ass. He squeezed with both hands, again finding that it drew a soft noise of pleasure from Dan. Either the other man really liked his ass grabbed, or he enjoyed the attention from Lucas. Both ideas were equally enticing, and Lucas brought him closer, catching Dan's mouth with his own.

The sweet taste of whatever Dan had been drinking hit his tongue as they slid over one another. Their mouths worked together, a point of heat and pleasure as Lucas rubbed and gripped the man's ass. He barely noticed the music anymore as Dan squirmed and wriggled, pushing back into the kiss with a passion that Lucas hadn't felt from another person in years.

He hadn't noticed what the other man had been up to in his movements until he felt cool air and then a warm hand brush against his cock. Lucas let out a low groan of pleasure as Dan stroked him, just as expertly and sensually as before.

"I think it's bigger than last time," Dan noted with a chuckle as he broke the kiss. "Which is saying something."

Lucas flushed at the praise. "I'm uh, less nervous this time."

"Good."

"Is this normal for a private dance?"

Dan laughed, slipping away from Lucas but never removing his hand from his cock. "It can be, all depends. But there are other things that happen in this room."

Lucas's mouth went dry as he watched Dan kneel on the floor before him. "Oh?"

"Yeah," Dan said, easing forward and hesitating.

Lucas knew what he was doing, and for a moment, he was filled with warmth and gratitude toward the other man. Dan had no fear of trying to push Lucas, get him to go past his limit and see what was on the other side. Yet, he was simultaneously conscientious about what he was doing, making sure he didn't go *too* far. It was an awkward dance that Dan somehow managed to pull off perfectly.

A nod from Lucas was all it took and Dan all but dived forward. Warmth wrapped around his cock, but Lucas didn't know if it was the sensation or the sight of Dan's freshly kissed lips wrapping around his cock that drew a strangled noise of pleasure from him.

Just as with the hand-job in the car, Dan was as meticulous and expert with his mouth. Lucas vaguely found himself comparing it to someone familiar with computers and, upon getting a new one, carefully went through the new device to find out what worked the same as the last one and what was new or improved.

He was more than impressed with how much of his cock Dan could fit into his mouth and throat. The squeeze of the man's throat muscles was pleasant, sending light but erotic tingles up and down his spine. The swirl of the man's tongue around the head of his cock drew a moan from him.

But the real kicker came when he felt the lightest brush of teeth over the head of his cock. Not nearly enough to be painful, but enough to jerk a much more significant groan from him without thought.

Dan drew back, grinning. "I love that you don't hold back. I know exactly when I'm doing something right."

Lucas didn't have the time to cobble together what few remaining functioning brain cells he had left to form an answer. Dan was right back at it, gripping the base of Lucas's cock and stroking it in rhythm with his mouth. With startling speed, the man managed to fit together a routine that had Lucas gaping down at him, holding onto the man's shoulders as he was pulled along for the ride.

Constant strokes from the man's hand, a dip to let the head of Lucas's cock be squeezed by Dan's throat muscles. A swift retreat, letting his tongue slide around and his teeth gently slide over. It was an impressive routine and an impromptu one at that.

Lucas could barely keep up, his brain firing rapidly as he tried to figure out how the hell Dan was doing what he was doing. It was not his first blow-job but damned if he'd met someone who had been so quick, or so intent, on picking up what the right pleasure combination was.

Lucas was helpless to stop the oncoming orgasm that was tightening his leg muscles and hardening his stomach. And while he suspected what Dan's reaction would be, he did his best to warn the other man what was coming. The only response he got was a flash of Dan's eyes up to him, locking onto Lucas's.

The simple act of eye contact was enough for Lucas and he cried out, not caring if there was even the remotest chance of being overheard. His eyes remained on Dan's face as the man kept his mouth wrapped around him. His cock pulsed as he pumped down into the man's throat, with Dan slipping his mouth down more to take Lucas even further as he came hard.

Lucas slumped back as the remainder of his strength left him. Sweat beaded on his forehead, and his chest was heaving. Dan's mouth slid off him carefully before even more gently tucking Lucas back into his underwear.

Lucas looked up at the speaker, squinting as he realized what song was playing. "Is this Pour Some Sugar on Me?"

Dan chuckled, picking himself up to flop down onto the couch beside him. "It most certainly is."

"You really weren't kidding about having something cliché to play," Lucas said, looking down to see the front of Dan's underwear straining.

Dan leaned back, closing his eyes with a smile. "I did warn you."

"You did," Lucas agreed, though his mind was on the other man.

In all his previous imaginings, he had never once considered what it would be like to touch anything but Dan's ass, let alone the rest of him. Then again, he hadn't considered allowing the man to jerk or suck him off either, and those two things had been winners.

With a deep breath, he reached down and cupped the other man's crotch. Dan's eyes flashed open but it was the only reaction he gave. Well, except for the twitch of his cock against Lucas's palm.

It was warm, and Lucas was relieved to find his fingers were steady as he carefully peeled back the underwear to reveal Dan's cock. Before he could second guess himself, he wrapped his hand around the shaft. Dan was burning hot in his hand, and the tip was shining from the excitement, making him leak.

As much as he wanted to warn that he wouldn't be very good, Lucas didn't trust whatever might spill out of his mouth. Instead, he tried to do his best to emulate what Dan had done before and find out what worked for him. It wasn't the easiest, and he felt clumsy as he stroked the man, absurdly delighted when Dan gave a soft whimper when Lucas's thumb rubbed along the underside of his cock.

Lucas continued, listening to the deepening of Dan's breathing as he tried to return the favor. When he turned to ask the other man if he was doing alright, Dan leaned in and kissed him fiercely. There was the same passion as before, but there was a desperation in that kiss that hadn't been there before. Dan's mouth was hot against his, and he could feel the man's cock jerking in his grip.

Dan gave a low noise, strangled and shaky, his hips pushing up into Lucas's hand. Warmth ran over his fingers as Dan came, the smaller man gripping Lucas harder and kissing him soundly. He felt the tremors of pleasure run through Dan as his body finally gave out and he let go of Lucas's mouth with a pant.

"You didn't have to do that," Dan told him, his gaze hazy and unfocused.

Lucas looked down at his cum covered hand. "I wanted to."

"I can't argue with that," Dan said, leaning his head on Lucas's shoulder and sighing pleasantly. "Can't argue with that at all."

Lucas stared at his hand longer. It wasn't really any different than coming on himself, though he wasn't quite sure if he was ready to risk a taste test. Still, he had discovered that receiving pleasure from Dan was quite fun and that giving it to him, while not as physically pleasurable, was still fun as hell too.

"I'm still not putting the brakes on," Lucas told him.

Dan shifted beside him, turning his brown eyes up to Lucas. "What does that mean?"

"I don't want anything...not the whole thing," Lucas sputtered, realizing how it could have been interpreted.

Dan laughed, kissing Lucas's shoulder. "Okay, so no anal, got ya."

"Thank you," Lucas said, touched by the small gesture of affection. "But...if you're okay with it. I don't mind...continuing this. We both seem to be enjoying it."

Dan watched his face, expression careful but curious. "That is definitely true. So, friends with benefits then?"

"I guess that would be the way to put it," Lucas told him. "I've never had one before."

Dan's mouth twitched but remained neutral. "I have. It's fun."

"And you'd be okay with that?" Lucas asked, not wanting the man to feel like he had to.

Dan chuckled, kissing Lucas once more. "Look, we're both having fun, right? And if we're both having fun, then we should keep having fun. No harm in that. So we'll keep the gas pedal in my control and the steering and brakes in yours."

"You can...take the steering wheel sometimes too," Lucas told him.

Dan hummed. "A top that likes a bossy bottom, good...good."

"I don't know what that means."

Dan only laughed, the sound making Lucas smile. "It just means that whatever happens over the next few weeks should be fun for us both. However long it goes on for."

Lucas liked the sound of it, even as he wondered just how long it would be.

DAN

Day One

"WELL, WELL," Dan said, leaning on the bar where he'd been doing inventory. "Look what the cat dragged in."

Lucas flashed him a smile, shaking his head. "In case it slipped your notice, I was supposed to be here this afternoon. There were a few things I needed to talk to Mr. Morales about with regard to the property and the paperwork Kimberly sent over."

"Alas," Dan said with mock regret. "Rico won't be in until this evening.

Lucas frowned. "I thought he and I had an arrangement. Did I have the wrong day?"

Dan laughed, shaking his head. "More like he just forgot. And there's no way in hell anyone here is going to wake him up to tell him a lawyer wants to speak to him. No offense."

Lucas shook his head, giving him a wry smile. "I'm a lawyer. The only time people are happy to see me is if they're in jail, or I can promise they're going to be free of all charges."

"See, that's where you went wrong with a career choice," Dan told him, writing on the nearby clipboard. "Because when I do my job, people are always happy to see me."

"I simply cannot imagine why," Lucas said sarcastically. "Perhaps it's just a fluke or your stunning personality."

"Are you trying to say I don't have a stunning personality?" Dan asked with an arched brow.

"Is this a trap I smell?" Lucas asked, raising a brow. "Because I'll have you know, I'm not falling for it."

"Oh, that's a shame," Dan said as he opened another cooler.

"But I will say that I most certainly find your personality to be endearing and comforting," Lucas told him as he leaned on the edge of the bar and watched him.

Dan smiled at that, warmed by the compliment. "You know, you are a very good complimenter. I hope you know that."

"I don't think that's a word, but I'll accept it with thanks anyway."

"How gracious of you."

"I am the rare, benevolent and kind sort of lawyer."

It was fun to see more of Lucas's personality come out in little bits and pieces. Much like Mateo, Lucas could deliver a joke with a deadpan tone. Dan had grown used to it and had a good feel for when Lucas was simply being dry. But there was still some of the playfulness, even silliness in the way Lucas joked, apparently not as super serious as he made himself out to be.

"I wasn't aware those types of lawyers existed," Dan told him, turning to check the rack of liquor bottles.

"They've been known to pop up from time to time," Lucas told him, his voice slowly trailing off.

Dan glanced over his shoulder and found Lucas's eyes dart up to his face. He smiled at the man, having a good idea where the man's eyes had been moments before. For someone who was so big on self-control and organized everything, Lucas's brain apparently went crazy when he was around something that turned him on. And Dan would be lying if he tried to claim it wasn't supremely flattering to know that the thing that turned the guy on was him.

"I'll have to keep an eye out for any," Dan said, making a note of the bottles and the amount of liquor left in them.

"Speaking of," Lucas began, now just on the other side of the bar from where Dan stood. "How long are you going to be doing inventory?"

Dan shrugged. "Could be another hour or two. Really I'm just doing it to get it out of the way."

"Well, if there's no rush, what would you say to lunch?"

"With you?"

Lucas snorted. "Yes, with me. It appears I have a rather large gap in my schedule since Mr. Morales decided to stand me up. What better way to fill in the time than with someone whose company I enjoy?"

Dan didn't even have to consider it. He set the clipboard aside and turned to Lucas with a grin. "Fine, it's a date."

Lucas was half a foot from him, leaning on the bar and giving him the strangest smile. "So it is."

DAY **Eight**

. . .

IT HAD ONLY BEEN a week since the first one, but the occasional shared lunch was becoming something of a habit for them. Well, it was lunch for the early riser Lucas and closer to breakfast for Dan, but he didn't mind. Working late hours, he was long since used to treating the first meal of his day as breakfast, even if it was a roast beef sandwich and chips from a local deli.

It was growing warmer every day and while Dan loved walking in the sunlight, he appreciated the moments where their quiet stroll put them under the shade of the trees. The section of Greenford where Nocturne sat was truly only busy when the sun went down and resembled a quiet little, well-mannered portion of the city during the day. It was the perfect place to walk around while munching on sandwiches and still have a measure of privacy.

"Rico did call you, right?" Dan asked, the thought suddenly occurring to him.

Lucas nodded, taking a bite of his own sandwich, laden heavily with house-made pastrami. "He did. And he had the most curious of questions to ask me in the process."

"Oh?" Dan said, peering up at the man curiously. "Like what?"

Lucas gave him a wink, swallowing his food. "Well, I can't really say."

"What?" Dan said indignantly. "Why the hell not? I thought I had permission to know things and make decisions."

"You do, but considering he is the actual client, he still has the right to keep things from you," Lucas explained. "And that particular discussion is one he...requested I keep from you."

Dan couldn't help but laugh at Lucas's tone. "Requested? You mean he swore at you and promised something awful, like beating you with your own briefcase, if you told me."

"Actually, he promised to shove it somewhere uncomfortable. I didn't feel obligated to tell him I don't *have* a briefcase and everything is on my tablet," Lucas said with a chuckle. "And for the record, he *does* want you to know, but on his terms."

"Man," Dan whined. "If that's the case, why even tell me in the first place? Why not just let him tell me when he wanted to tell me."

"Because it's not often I get a genuine reaction out of you when I'm teasing," Lucas said, and Dan noted the bastard had a devilish twinkle in his eyes as he took another bite.

Dan turned to him, scowling. "You are the worst."

"There is no way in hell or heaven that you did not endure far worse through the years of friendship with my brother," Lucas told him with a smirk. "But if you're going to rank me as worse than him, I'll take it as a compliment."

Dan held his frown. "You absolutely are."

"You trying to be intimidating and angry is actually a little cute," Lucas told him with a raised brow.

"You think I'm cute?" Dan asked, eyes widening.

Much as he expected, Lucas's face colored and all cockiness and impishness left his expression. The confident lawyer had left the building, and instead, the man who didn't know what to do or say when it came to Dan had returned.

"See," Dan said with a grin. "Now watching you turn into a nervous schoolboy because you gave me a nice compliment, *that* is funny."

Lucas huffed, shaking his head. "Behave yourself."

"Or what, you'll punish me?"

"Oh ho, very funny. And not at all transparent."

Dan tried a new tactic. "Or what, you'll drag me to a secluded corner of one of the empty parks around here to let me have my way with you?"

Lucas froze as he bundled up the wax paper that had once held his sandwich. His green eyes swiveled to Dan's face, and at that moment, Dan knew he had the other man. It had been days since the last time they'd done anything, and if Dan was coming to know Lucas as much as he thought he did, he was pretty sure the man hadn't taken care of his own release in the meantime.

"Damn you," Lucas grumbled, turning to walk away.

Incidentally, he was walking toward one of the previously mentioned empty parks. Dan followed, a wicked grin on his face as he went.

DAY FIFTEEN

BEING CALLED into Rico's office wasn't unusual, but the moment Dan walked in, he sensed something was different about this impromptu meeting. Rico wasn't staring at something, there wasn't a drink in his hand, and his expression was thoughtful rather than the irritated scowl that normally sat on his face.

"Oh God," Dan said when he spotted him. "Who died?"

Rico looked up thoughtfully, motioning to the only other seat in the office, one that rarely got used. "Sit."

"Oh God," Dan repeated in a worried tone, stomach twisting lightly. "Did someone actually die?"

"No," Rico told him, his familiar scowl returning. "I wanted to talk to your ass about something that's been on my mind."

"Is that supposed to make me feel better?" Dan asked as he sat down.

Rico pulled out a piece of paper and set it atop the mess of other papers strewn about the desk. "I've been going over this list of shit I'd have to pay for to get the new place."

Dan recognized his handwriting, tidy and a strange mix of print and cursive. "Right, is it too much?"

Rico snorted, leaning back in his seat. "No. I can handle it. Sure as hell will sting a bit in the pocketbook, but I can do it without going under. I had another idea."

"Is there something wrong with the building?" Dan asked, realizing he hadn't checked up on Rico to see how things were going and that none of his recent conversations with Lucas had been about the deal.

Rico shook his head. "Building's fine, and I'm sure you aren't wrong about how much that bitch is gonna cost either. But I got to thinking about a way that I didn't have to fork over as much and also not have to worry about how the place is gonna get run at the same time. Asked that lawyer what he thought about my idea too."

"Lucas?"

"Yeah, the pretty boy you've been hanging around with for the past couple of weeks."

Dan frowned at him. "He mentioned you talked to him about something."

Rico's eyes narrowed. "That fucker."

"He didn't tell me what, though," Dan told him quickly. "He only told me he'd talked to you and couldn't tell me. Little shit also told me he'd only told me because he knew it would drive me crazy."

Rico snorted. "I guess he knows you pretty well."

"He's an ass. And so are you."

Rico smirked at that. "Right, well, I presented the idea to him and he said I could do what I wanted with the arrangement."

"That sounds like him, perfectly professional," Dan said with a laugh.

"Right and I told him to give me his personal opinion, not his stupid ass lawyer one."

"And what'd he say?"

"He said that as far as he could tell, it would be a fantastic idea. Gave a list of reasons why and I gotta say, the man knows his shit. Or at least knows you."

"Uh, can we get to the point where I know what you're talking about?" Dan asked nervously.

"Partners," Rico told him simply, tapping the page of expenses. "Honestly, if you can afford it, go half in on buying the place and the expenses. You do half, I do half, and we both own it and split the profits."

"I...what?" Dan asked, shocked.

Rico nodded. "I can't be fucked to run another place. Sounds like a reason to walk into traffic if you ask me. So it'd be you in charge, doing all the stuff you've already done here, and me letting you do your thing. And, if you get enough to buy me out in the future, I'll take that too. Don't matter much to me."

Dan shook his head, thoughts spinning. "You want me to partner...and buy you out?"

"Eh," Rico said with a shrug. "The extra club was just an idea I had and it kinda ran outta my hands. And shit, it would probably take a while for you to get the place making enough for you to buy me out, so I'd still get plenty of time to make money of my own."

Dan stared down at the list, heart thumping. "And Lucas told you this would be a good idea?"

"He told me that if I was willing to leave you in charge of shit like Nocturne, and even this deal, it meant I must know you aren't gonna fuck things up," Rico said with a shrug. "And what can I say? He's right. You might be a goofy motherfucker, but you keep this place running smoothly when you're in charge."

Dan didn't know how to react to the information. Not only did Rico actually believe in his ability to do things effectively, but Lucas had outright supported him. It was one thing for the man to say nice things to Dan's face, but to turn around and say them to someone he barely knew? It warmed him to know that someone outside of his very small circle of trust believed in him just as much as those inside it did.

"Uh," Dan managed, looking down at the sheet of paper. "Do I get time to think about this?"

Rico snorted, waving him off. "Think about it all you want. I'm going through with buying the place and doing all this shit. So if you decide you want in halfway through, you just give me what half of the previous costs were and we can fuck around and find out what to do from there. I don't give a shit."

"Kinda thinking you do," Dan said with a smile. "You knew damn well that I was wondering what to do with myself. What I was going to do after I had to stop performing. And now you're offering me the chance to start not only new but strong."

Rico rolled his eyes. "Don't get sentimental on me. You start fucking up, especially because you're making goo-goo eyes at the straight boy, and I'll leave you in the dust and not feel bad about it."

"Sure, Rico," Dan said with a smile, standing up. "Whatever you say."

"Yeah, and I say go make sure the dressing room doesn't look like shit. You fuckers trash the place every night," Rico said, pointing toward the door.

Dan went, knowing Rico's patience for any more emotion was all but spent. He definitely was going to check on the dressing room, but first, he was going to make a call.

A certain someone deserved a proper thank you.

Day Twenty-Two

DAN HAD FULLY KNOWN what would happen after being invited to Lucas's house. He was more amused by how Lucas went through the motions of inviting him in and putting something on the TV to play as background noise as they sat and talked. Not that Dan minded, he was steadily growing to enjoy their conversations without the presence of anything sexual. That it turned into sex eventually was a nice bonus, but it didn't have to happen.

He had expected Lucas to live in some huge and sprawling place, or at least one of considerable size. Instead, when he drove up, he found the man lived in what Dan could only refer to as 'the cutest little cottage he'd ever seen.' He had, of course, made sure to mention it in hearing range of Lucas, earning him a little shake of the man's head, but a small smile as well.

It was made to look as though the outer walls were made of heavy stone. Vines crept up the side of the house, trailing down to lush and rich flowerbeds that were neatly tended. Dan had no idea how the man found the time to get any gardening done, but he'd clearly inherited his mother's love of all things growing and colorful.

The inside was what he could only think of as modern rustic. Wood and stone made up a lot of the materials, from the wooden tables with shining stone surfaces to the fireplace on the back wall of the living room, cleaned but stacked with fresh wood. The furniture was much the same, though it was wood and dark leather, the faint smell of smoke lingering on them.

Dan had ended up on the couch with Lucas, curled on his side, his head on the man's lap. He had been surprised the first time Lucas had responded well to overt affection. Such as when Dan took his hand as they walked through a quiet, sunny park or letting him lay his head on Lucas's arm while they ate lunch together on a bench. It had felt almost completely natural to lay his head in the man's lap as they watched a crime drama on the TV, with Lucas's hand eventually coming to rest on his head.

"You know," Dan said, stirring out of his thoughts. "Considering you deal with crime and criminals all the time, I'd think you'd hate this kind of show."

"Are you kidding me? Sometimes I wish courtroom drama was like this," Lucas chuckled. "It would make my job so much more exciting. I don't hate these shows because they're unrealistic. I envy it."

Dan snorted, absently tracing circles on Lucas's thigh with his finger. "Need a little excitement in your life?"

Lucas pulled gently on his hair, the strands falling loosely through his grip. "I might have denied it before, but having you come around and pull me along for the ride has shown me that maybe I was protesting too much."

"I'm not sure if that sounded like a compliment. I hope you meant it as such," Dan laughed.

"I meant it," Lucas said with sudden earnestness. "If someone had told me I'd have someone come into my life that would…push me to stop being so static, to at least branch out a little, I would have scoffed."

"You say that like you're going out and skydiving or base jumping or something," Dan said, a little pleased by the conversation.

"No, it's not that. And it's not even the sexual things we've been doing that I'm talking about. Though that does play a part."

Dan had noticed, though he'd kept his mouth shut, that Lucas had grown more and more comfortable mentioning or talking overtly about sex as time went on. He didn't have his younger brother's outlandish and very open approach to sex, but he was open, just private and slow to warm to it. There was something special about watching the man slowly come out of his shell, as though Dan were being allowed to witness a rare event.

"Well, I'm glad I was able to help," Dan told him, meaning it. "It's always nice to know when you've been making a positive impact on someone's life."

Lucas brushed his fingers along Dan's neck and down to his collarbone. "And I've been thinking."

"Oh?"

"About the only brake I put on before."

Ah, right, the anal.

"What about it?" Dan asked, resisting the urge to look up at Lucas and potentially make the situation a little too intense for the man.

"I would like to take those brakes off if you want."

Dan finally did get up at that, sensing Lucas wasn't

nearly as nervous and awkward as he'd suspected. "You want to fuck me."

The words had an immediate effect. Lucas didn't blush this time, but his jaw set and he watched the man's nostrils flare. He could have looked pissed, but Dan knew that look by now.

Lucas was turned on.

"If you're willing," Lucas told him. "I've...never done anal, let alone with a guy."

Dan grinned. "Well, why don't you show me where you keep that bed of yours and we can change that."

LUCAS

Lucas took hold of Dan's hand once he'd finished speaking, rose from the couch and escorted him back toward the bedroom. His heart was thundering away, but he didn't really mind. It seemed like every time he and Dan did anything sexual or intimate, his heart was always pounding ferociously. Lucas had slowly come to expect it, accept it, and even look forward to it.

Yes, there was definitely anxiety and nerves, but it was excitement too. Sex with Dan excited him, the man himself caused excitement. And that meant Lucas wanted to do things right, so, of course, he was going to worry. Yet every time, Lucas walked away from intimacy with Dan feeling warm, accepted, and like he'd managed to perform his role spectacularly.

"Quick question," Dan said once they reached the bedroom. "We are going to need a couple of things you might not have used in your past relationships."

Lucas turned to face him. The phrasing of the sentence struck him as both strange and somehow comforting. Before he could even bother to process that sudden realization, he was stopped as Dan pulled his shirt up, over his head, and tossed it on the ground. It wasn't the man's ass, but Lucas still drank in the sight, realizing how familiar it had become, yet losing none of its impact as he felt his pants tighten.

"I took care of that," Lucas told him, eyes sweeping over Dan's narrow shoulders and tapered waist, knowing he would find out what it looked like beneath him very soon.

Dan grinned at that. "You sly dog, you've been thinking about this for a while."

"If I hadn't been thinking about it heavily, you would have wondered if something was wrong with me," Lucas said, reaching out to bring Dan closer.

"That," Dan began, popping the first few buttons on Lucas's shirt open. "Is very true."

Once, he might have found it both strange and thrilling to kiss the other man and strip one another down. The first time they'd ever been completely naked around one another had been in the dressing room of Nocturne a couple of weeks back. The presence of another naked male body against his had been weird at first, but that thought was quickly lost when Dan pressed up against him, kissing him soundly.

The effect of Dan was much the same, though it no longer felt weird. If anything, the press of the man's chest against his, his hard cock squeezed between their two bodies, all just added to the moment, thrilling him.

They tumbled onto the bed, Dan's mouth still pressed against Lucas's hungrily. Lucas grabbed the man's hips as Dan fell atop him, rutting his cock up between the man's legs and against his ass. He had grown to appreciate several parts of Dan's body, but he was never quite going to forget his favorite.

"Bedside table?" Dan mumbled against his lips.

"Yeah," Lucas told him breathlessly, heart firing up once again.

They were close enough that Dan only needed to roll slightly to the side to reach in and grab the new pack of condoms and bottle of lube. The bottle made a sharp cracking noise as it was opened, and Dan tossed one of the condoms onto the bed beside them.

"You sure about this?" Dan asked, cocking his head.

That made Lucas smile because it used to be him asking that. "Absolutely."

"Ooh, a definitive answer, I like it," Dan said with a wink.

Lucas watched as the other man rose up to kneel on either side of Lucas's hips, spreading the clear fluid onto his fingers. Carefully, Dan rested the bottle against Lucas's side before reaching behind him. Lucas's eyes flit between the man's hand as it disappeared behind him and up to Dan's face.

Dan hesitated and then smirked. "I have a better idea."

Lucas blinked, watching as Dan rolled off him and onto his back. He got up, curious to know what Dan was doing and then froze as Dan reached down to push his fingers inside himself.

He knew there was prep involved, but Lucas had not been ready to watch as Dan slowly began to fuck himself with his fingers. Lucas knelt, sitting back on his legs as Dan managed to push another finger inside. Cock straining before him, Lucas watched, enraptured as Dan made a show of the entire affair.

Lucas was torn between watching the man's face as he made low noises adding a third finger or watching as his fingers slipped inside. The whole affair had him suddenly burning with a need to put himself in place of the fingers and hope he could draw even more noises out of the other man.

Dan smirked at him, drawing his fingers out of himself and pointing at Lucas. "Your turn."

Lucas nearly forgot the condom in his haste to take his turn. They both had a chuckle as Lucas leaned back to open the condom in a hurry and roll it down over his cock. Another helping of lube was added and he leaned over, putting his arms on either side of Dan as he pushed forward.

Despite all the prep work, there was still a moment of resistance as he tried to slide his hips forward. It was only a few seconds, and suddenly tight heat wrapped around the head of his cock. Dan's mouth fell open as Lucas slid further into him, back arching slightly as he groaned.

"Oh, shit," Dan groaned, reaching up to hold onto Lucas.

He was nearly in and froze. "You okay?"

"Oh, I'm already better than okay," Dan chuckled.

"It doesn't hurt?"

"A little, but in the best way possible."

Lucas wasn't going to argue with the man. He trusted Dan wasn't just saying that to make him feel better. Continuing his way forward, he got the last couple of inches snugly inside the other man, unable to help his moan of pleasure as he felt Dan wrapped completely around him.

Although he knew he should move, and soon, Lucas had to take a deep breath and steady himself. He had strongly suspected that being inside Dan was going to feel incredible, but he hadn't been prepared for the reality. He couldn't decide if it was the grip or the heat that had him, but he knew damn well the man's flushed features as he stared up at him in erotic anticipation was not helping.

The grip was still strong when he eased his hips back and pushed down into the man. Both of them groaned as Lucas continued, trying to build up a rhythm and not get completely lost in the sensation. Dan's legs wrapped around his waist, drawing him in deeper every time he thrust down into him.

Lucas shifted forward, adjusting their position slightly, forcing Dan to raise his hips. The next thrust drew a harsh noise from Dan, the man's mouth falling open. Lucas did it again and again, drawing even louder noises from the other man.

Lucas picked up the pace, all but shoving himself completely into the other man with each thrust. Dan's grip on him became fierce, his cock leaking copiously against his stomach as Lucas drove himself inside him, slamming into the place that sent Dan into a frenzy of pleasure. The man squirmed and bucked against him, wanting more of him, something Lucas was all too willing to give.

Sweat trickled down his back, beading on his brow, and it coated Dan's hairless chest. Pleasure zinged through him, filling Lucas as he continued to pound down into the man, helpless to do anything but give Dan exactly what he wanted.

Without warning, Dan reached between them, gripping his cock and giving it a few jerks. The grip around Lucas's cock became ironclad, nearly holding him in place as Dan's muscles spasmed. He watched as Dan cried out, arching his back to push up against Lucas to keep him as deep as possible and splatter his stomach as he came. Lucas was right behind him, bowing forward to cry out into the man's neck as his own orgasm took him, his cock pulsing deep inside him.

It took Lucas a couple of minutes to find the strength to

get rid of the condom and fetch a towel to clean the other man up with. For his part, Dan continued to laze around on the bed, looking a little out of it as he stared up at the ceiling.

"You okay?" Lucas asked him as he wiped the man down carefully.

Dan swiveled his head toward him, reached up and pulled Lucas down to kiss him. There was heat to the kiss, but it was a little weak and hazy. It was the kiss of someone who was well satiated by what had just happened, and it sent a warm flutter through Lucas's chest.

"For someone who's never done that before," Dan told him. "You sure as hell should keep doing it."

Lucas leaned down, kissing the man gently. "After that? I'll be sure to."

"I'm going to hold you to that."

"Good."

There was a pause and then Dan spoke again.

"Hey, Lucas?"

"Yeah?"

"Do you mind if I crash here tonight?"

Lucas cocked his head. Absently, he ran a finger down Dan's cheek and across his neck. They'd never been to one another's house before, and they'd never fucked before either. Now Dan was asking to do one more thing they hadn't done and stay the night.

He could imagine Dan stretched out across his bed, bathed in morning light as he slept peacefully. Lucas was also pretty sure that the affectionate Dan was a cuddler and would probably love being wrapped up by the bigger Lucas, held as they talked or perhaps even slept.

"Of course you can," Lucas told him.

DAY **Thirty-Four**

LUCAS FOUND himself wishing he could get out of the office. Rico Morales was not a man who was all that fond of keeping things neat and orderly. He had despised the sight of the office when he'd first entered, and his feelings about it weren't any better now that Dan wasn't included.

"So, if you just sign these," Lucas told him, handing over a stack of papers. "You'll be all set to go. I'll deal with the rest."

"Thought you were all about the electronic," Rico said, looking over the papers.

"Usually, but not everything needs to be electronic, and this can expedite the process a little more," Lucas told him.

Which wasn't normally true. Electronic paperwork made the system a lot smoother and faster. The problem was, Mr. Morales was not exactly on top of everything if it wasn't directly attributed to Nocturne. It had been Dan's idea to have Mr. Morales deal with physical paperwork, and when Lucas was present. Otherwise, Dan would have to be the one to hound the man until he finally capitulated and signed everything.

"You two behaving in here?" a familiar warm voice asked from behind Lucas.

Lucas couldn't help his smile as he turned around to spy Dan watching them. The man was wearing a low-slung pair of basketball shorts and a muscle tee with slits down the side. With the angle Dan was standing, it was all too easy to see the man's hips.

"Just going through some paperwork," Lucas told him,

polite as ever because they had an audience. "We're on the last leg of purchasing the building and I figured Mr. Morales would want to get through this as quickly as possible."

"And he's right," Mr. Morales said, slapping the pages back on the side of the desk where Lucas sat. "Because I don't want to keep looking at all that legal shit."

"That was," Lucas began as he looked down at the papers, looking through them. "Fast."

Dan chuckled. "Told you. Make him do it face to face and he'll get it out of the way to make sure he's not annoyed about it anymore."

"You told me it made things faster to do it on actual paper," Mr. Morales accused Lucas.

Lucas gave him a smile, tucking the paperwork away in his bag. "That's true. I just didn't feel the need to specify *why* it would make it faster."

"Ugh," the man grunted, standing up. "I knew letting the two of you be around one another would be trouble."

"He says for the first time ever," Dan remarked with a wicked grin.

"Get out of my way," Mr. Morales barked at Dan. "Unlike you, I have shit to do around here."

Dan stepped into the office, out of the grumpy man's way, chuckling as they could hear him grumbling all the way down the hallway. "He's so good at pretending like he doesn't like me."

"It *is* a remarkably good act," Lucas agreed, setting his things aside.

"And how's my busy lawyer?" Dan asked, tilting his head.

Lucas smiled at the slightly possessive language. He knew Dan meant it affectionately and without any demands placed upon Lucas. But it still made him smile, and he reached out to hook a finger into the waistband of Dan's shorts through the slit in the side.

"Strangely," Lucas said in a low voice. "My days have been getting better and better lately. No idea why."

"Careful," Dan warned him. "You know what happens when you feed a cat, right?"

"I do."

"Being affectionate has the same effect on me."

Lucas laughed, tugging playfully at Dan's shorts. "I think I'll manage to survive."

Dan hummed before standing on the tips of his toes to kiss Lucas. In all fairness, Lucas had no problem if the man decided he wanted to linger for longer. The two of them always managed to enjoy themselves when they were with one another, with or without clothes.

In truth, he'd grown very used to Dan's presence in his day-to-day life. If they weren't running into one another because Lucas had to stop by Nocturne for business, it was their frequent lunches or the time they spent together when they were both free. Dan was steadily becoming a fixture in his life, and Lucas was beginning to wonder just how he'd managed to go without him for so long.

"And if you keep tugging on those shorts, you're going to get something else," Dan told him as they separated.

"Why do you think I was tugging on them?" Lucas asked, slipping his hand into the man's shorts, delighted to find there was nothing else between him and Dan's ass as he grabbed it.

"Horn dog," Dan said, with all the affection he could muster.

Privately, Lucas thought that the other man was a little surprised to find Lucas was actually a sexual person.

Though, he didn't blame Dan for being surprised. He had already admitted he wasn't that great at taking care of himself in that regard, and he'd been more than a little reserved when he and Dan had started down this strange but wonderful path. There was always a little something holding him back, and if it wasn't the fact that they barely knew one another at first, it was the fact that Lucas had really not been all that confident when it came to sleeping with another man.

And though he wouldn't call himself an expert, after only a handful of weeks of hand-jobs and blow-jobs and just under two of actual fucking, he was far less reserved. Though he wasn't surprised, he was delighted to find that Dan was just as willing to have some fun, whether it be for the night or in the few minutes they had of spare time.

For Lucas, it was a lot like discovering a new toy to play with. Except that toy also came attached with Dan's personality and company. Lucas loved making the man come, watching as his cock slid into him and grabbing him as they drove one another to orgasm. Yet it was the lazy smile on Dan's face afterward, the laugh he'd make in the middle of sex if Lucas brushed his side too hard, and the way he looked sprawled on Lucas's couch, clothed or unclothed, as he made himself at home, that really made Lucas's day.

"Well," Dan said, grinning. "How about you and I go upstairs? I hear those private dance rooms have the most scandalous things hiding away."

"And how could I say no to an offer like that?" Lucas asked with a laugh. "By all means, show me the dirty secrets."

DAY FORTY-SIX

SUNDAY EVENINGS HAD ALWAYS BEEN his favorite time of the week. As much as his family drove him crazy, it was always nice to sit down with them and reconnect after a long week of work.

As always, dinner had been prepared by Christopher and his mother, while Mateo and himself were always in charge of cleaning up afterward. Both Christopher and their mother had disappeared somewhere in the house, while Lucas and Mateo had gone to the back porch to watch the sun set and drink a couple of beers in comfortable silence.

"You know," Lucas said, taking a sip. "I almost took an offer out in Chicago at a different firm."

"Really?" Mateo asked. "I never knew that. I just remember you spending days on end trying to make up your mind."

"I almost took it. I mean, it was a great offer and I couldn't have been happier," Lucas said as he watched the sky burn with orange and red streaks. "But damn, I would have missed it here. I might not have even known how much I would have missed it. But sitting here, right now? I'm glad I stayed."

Mateo peered over at him, dark eyes practically burrowing into the side of Lucas's head. "Well, aren't we feeling sentimental?"

Lucas laughed. "Only a little. Hard not to when you've got a sight like this."

He was taking another drink when Mateo spoke. "Or when you're nailing my best friend."

Lucas's throat seized, spitting the beer out onto the

porch as he coughed. He could feel his face turning red as he sputtered, trying to wipe off his pant leg and simultaneously glare at his brother.

"*What* is wrong with you?" Lucas demanded when he finally found his breath.

Mateo, utterly unfazed, took another drink and shrugged. "I mean, if you're going to nail my best friend and former partner, I'm going to have something to say about it."

Lucas's head snapped toward his brother. "Your *what*?"

Mateo looked at him in amusement. "You didn't know?" He thought about it and shook his head. "No, I guess you wouldn't know, would you? Funny thing about Dan, he's pretty liberal about sex, but he's not one to kiss and tell. Didn't even tell me sometimes, so that makes sense."

Lucas was both trying to make sense of the idea that Dan and Mateo had slept together while also trying desperately not to picture anything. "No, he never mentioned it. I assume he thought I would find it a little strange."

"Probably. Good for him. Nice to know he's still able to read people."

"Wait, how do you know?"

Mateo gave him a sidelong glance and a smirk. "If you guys are going to screw in Nocturne when it's closed, remember there are other people there too. Glam caught you guys in the dressing room."

"Never pegged him as a gossip," Lucas grumbled, thinking of the big and normally quiet man.

"Oh, he's awful," Mateo laughed. "If you get to be friends with him, he will spill all sorts of shit that he's seen and heard over the years. Seriously, he's worse than Donna when it comes to gossiping."

Lucas glanced at his brother, nervously fidgeting with the bottle. "And none of this...bothers you?"

Mateo frowned at him. "Bother me? Why, because I slept with him? Man, that was *years* ago, and it was never anything serious. We both knew from the start that it was just friends with benefits and wouldn't be anything else. There's nothing there but brotherly love between him and me now."

Lucas grew quiet as he wondered if that's what Dan saw in them. They *had* agreed to make their relationship exactly that, friends with benefits. Yet, the title of their arrangement sounded strange and foreign to his thoughts. It felt like he was reducing what Dan was to something simple and easily discarded. The thought was an ugly one, and the beer turned slightly in his gut.

"Or are you asking me if I'm bothered that my big brother finally saw the light?" Mateo asked with a grin.

Lucas rolled his eyes. "Saw the light. You and Dan, you're both ridiculous. He referred to me as 'tragically straight' when I met him."

Mateo laughed. "Yeah, that sounds like Dan, alright. That man can get away with saying so much, and it's probably because he's just naturally adorable."

Lucas had to admit there was some truth to what his brother was saying. Though he didn't see it as 'seeing the light', he definitely understood why his brother was such a fan of being with other men. Most of that had to do with Dan, though, whose playful personality and friendly demeanor soothed something in Lucas, making it almost effortless to let his guard down and enjoy himself.

Mateo shrugged. "People aren't simple. They aren't black and white, and they're never going to be. I mean, just look at Chris's mom. She loves him and she *means* well with how she is, but at the same time, what she does is smothering, overcontrolling, and toxic."

"Are we comparing human sexuality to toxic co-dependent behavior now?" Lucas asked dryly.

"God, sometimes I forget how literal you are," Mateo snorted. "I just meant, things are always going to be gray with people. It's just how we're built. So yeah, maybe you have been hetero your whole life, and yet something about Dan just BOOM, tweaked that knob a little bit and then...well, you guys were slobbering on each other's knobs."

Lucas chose not to react to his brother's crude comment and focus on the actual conversation. "I might regret this, but I can tell you what first did it for me."

Mateo smirked. "His ass."

"How did you..."

Mateo held up his fingers as he made his point. "One, you're an ass man. Trust me, you're not as subtle as you think and don't think for one minute I didn't see that most of your exes had really nice asses. Two, I know what Dan's ass looks like, and it's a nice ass. And three, if you tell Chris I said that I'll give you all the explicit detail about something sexual between Dan and me to scar you for life."

Yeah, he really didn't need that thought in his head. Any more than he needed to wonder what he and Mateo were like as comparative lovers. Oh, the curiosity would sit there, but there was no way in hell he was going to ask Dan to compare them.

"Fine, fair enough," Lucas relented with a grunt. "But the ass isn't only what caught me."

"Oh?" Mateo asked, sounding intrigued. "So there's more than just getting caught?"

Lucas smiled, giving a light shrug. "He's a good man."

"He is. I'm happy to call him my best friend."

"He's got a very warm personality, and even from the

start, he was good at making me feel comfortable and got me to smile. He's good at filling silences but knows how to enjoy them too. He's been ridiculously patient with me and knows me so damn well sometimes that I don't know if I should appreciate it or be a little worried. I don't know. It's not just his ass, or the sex, both of which I...enjoy." He cleared his throat, really not willing to get into details with his brother or anyone. "But it's more than just...*that*."

"It's him," Mateo said simply. "The ass caught you, but the man kept you around."

"Succinct and surprisingly not all that crude for you," Lucas noted.

"So, when are you going to make it official?"

"Make what official?"

"You and Dan. You know, as a thing, a serious thing. Dating? Relationship? Ringing a bell here?"

Lucas froze, his brother's question sinking in with all the grace and speed of a plummeting boulder. He had not once considered the possibility of *dating* Dan before. It had always just been friendship with sex on the side, occasionally a lot of sex on the side. Sure they got along, hell, Lucas knew damn well he was incredibly fond of the man and would be heartbroken to lose someone like Dan from his life.

But to date him?

"Good God," Mateo groaned. "You're thinking about it now because you never thought about it before."

"No, I didn't," Lucas admitted quietly.

"I love you," Mateo told him fondly. "You get so caught up in things sometimes, you don't think to look ahead. But, while you're spending hours upon hours thinking about this 'bombshell' I just dropped on you, I really need you to remember what you just spouted off to me before I asked."

What? That Dan was a warm and wonderful person? That the more time Lucas spent around him, the more Lucas wanted to be around him? That the idea of treating Dan as something disposable made him feel queasy, and he thought friends with benefits was really a poor way of describing what was going on with them?

Oh.

"Oh," Lucas repeated aloud, quietly staring down at his beer.

"Yeah," Mateo told him, taking another drink. "Oh."

DAN

His nerves were going to get the best of him, and he quietly tried to get himself to calm down. Dan stood outside Rico's office, waiting for the man to stop yelling at one of the delivery companies so that he could talk to him. He had given a lot of thought to Rico's offer, considered the expenses and had made his decision. Which had sounded good at the time, but now that he was facing down having to give Rico the decision, his nerves were wire tight.

It wasn't helped by the fact that he was feeling the beginning of an end coming his way. He hadn't had the chance to really speak to Lucas in days, let alone see the man. The last time they'd talked had been when Lucas had chatted with him over the phone before saying he was off to the family dinner they all had every Sunday.

After that, the other man had been *very* quiet. There had been minimal texting between them, and the only phone call had been Lucas clarifying a point about the upcoming contract. There had been no surprise visits, no lunches, nothing.

Dan smiled sadly as he checked his phone and found

nothing. He had known it was more than likely that eventually, Lucas would bail. Once he'd had his fill, he would decide to move on before Dan tried to get too serious. He'd probably even found himself a girl already, ready to leave behind everything that had been between them.

The worst part was Dan knew he'd fucked up because there *was* something between them. Though he'd tried to leave his feelings at the door, he knew he'd failed at that miserably, probably from the very first time he'd kissed the other man. Lucas was sweet and gentle, but he was steady and confident, his eyes crinkled when he smiled, and Dan had grown to love the feel of the man's hand resting casually on his hip.

He'd made the number one mistake and let himself slowly fall for a straight guy.

"Dan!" Rico barked from the office. "I know you're out there lurking, get your ass in here and say whatever you came to say. Jesus Christ."

Dan rolled his eyes, stepping in. "Well, forgive me for being polite and letting you finish reaming poor Keith."

"If I was reaming him, he would know," Rico grumbled, tossing his phone onto a pile of candy wrappers.

"I'm not asking for clarification. I don't want to know," Dan said with a cringe.

Rico turned, raising an annoyed brow. "What do you want?"

Dan considered taking the chair for a moment before remaining standing. "I wanted to talk to you about the offer you made me."

Rico stopped fussing with the stack of papers and looked up. "And?"

Dan took a deep breath and nodded. "I want to go in half with you."

"You're sure?" Rico asked, raising a brow. "That's a pretty hefty price point, and we don't know how well the club will do."

"I know," Dan told him.

And he did too. He'd done the research, he'd looked into how places like clubs and bars typically did, and he'd tossed and turned over how much it was going to cost. Going in half was something he could do, though he was sure it was going to hurt him a hell of a lot more than it would hurt Rico. Still, he also knew it was a damned good opportunity and one that would create debt for him even if it went well.

"I'm sure," Dan told him.

Rico leaned back in his seat and nodded. "Alright, well, if you're going to be a part of this, you're going to take over for most of dealing with the repairs and whatnot. So, that means less time here dancing and more time dealing with paperwork and bullshit."

"I think I can manage," Dan told him.

"Yeah, I know *that*. Otherwise, I wouldn't have made you the offer in the first place," Rico told him with a sneer. "My point is you're not going to live off the basic stripper income if you're not actually stripping. So, you're getting bumped up to assistant manager and we'll give you a new wage. You can still strip though, might as well flaunt it while you got it."

Dan was taken aback. "Wait, seriously?"

"Why the fuck not? People still want to see your twink ass shaking all over the place."

"That's not what I meant, Rico?"

"What, I was going to make you do all this shit while I do as little as possible and *not* pay you for it? Fuck off Dan. I'm an asshole, not a bastard."

Dan wasn't even going to bother to ask how there was

that much of a difference. Rico would surely go into one of his infamous rants, clarifying his point, and Dan would still walk away not knowing what the difference was.

"I'll deal with that shit tomorrow," Rico muttered, moving the wrappers into the trash bin. "I'll have that lawyer of yours send over the paperwork he drew up for it already, just in case you did go through with it. So keep an eye on your email, alright?"

"Sure, Rico," Dan said, hardly believing what he'd just agreed to do.

"And," Rico shrugged, holding out his hand. "I know it's not official yet, but partners?"

Dan grinned, taking his hand and shaking it. "Partners it is."

"Fine, now get the hell out of my office. I have to make a few calls still and my phone has fucking disappeared again."

"Check the trash can," Dan told him as he backed out of the office.

"How the *fuck* did it get in there?" Rico growled as he fished the device out.

Dan went a few more feet down the hallway and leaned against the wall, taking a deep breath. He was thrilled at what he had done and freaked out about what was going to be expected of him. Although he'd taken over for Rico to run Nocturne for a week here and there, things were going to be completely different at this new club.

He wasn't going to just be some employee, he was going to be *the* employee. Hell, he was going to be a partner, having as much say in how things were done as Rico. Dan wouldn't have to worry about what his future would hold quite as much as before because he'd already be building his future. It was a terrifying prospect but damned if he wasn't thrilled at the chance to have just that.

His phone buzzed, and he picked it out of his pocket to read the message from Lucas.

Do you have free time tonight? I think it's long past time you and I talked.

His elation dimmed, and his chest tightened. He had known this would come eventually, but he wasn't ready for it to be so soon. Then again, perhaps it was best that it came before Dan well and truly got attached.

Yeah I got time

How about that little park over off of Oak St? Nine o'clock?

Yeah sure

Lucas didn't say anything else after that, but Dan figured the man would have plenty to say once they saw one another. With a heavy heart, he tucked his phone back in his pocket.

DAN ARRIVED at the park earlier than nine, but only by a few minutes. He walked into the small grassy area nestled between two sets of buildings. The sun was on its way down, lengthening the shadows of the trees and giving it a strange, almost hazy feel. It would have been a nice walk, as he strolled along the narrow path if it wasn't for the fact that he knew what he was walking into.

He'd spent the better part of the day preparing himself for the inevitable. Dan knew full well that it wasn't really going to help soften the blow, but at least he could know it was coming as best as possible. Maybe he could slip into Nocturne after it was all said and done and have a few drinks to ease the incoming heartache.

Dan stopped when he found Lucas sitting on top of a

picnic table just off the little path. The man's jacket was gone, and his tie was loose around his neck. He was peering up at the tree line as though watching the light begin to recede and the color of the setting sun explode across the horizon. The sight tugged at Dan's heartstrings, and he quickly did his best to tamp it down as he approached.

Lucas's head snapped to him when he heard his approach. He took a deep breath as if steadying himself and pointed toward the picnic table.

"Hey," Dan said as he took the seat, unconsciously putting space between them.

"Hey, how was your day?" Lucas asked, sounding more like a professional lawyer than someone who knew Dan.

"It was good," Dan told him, leaving out his agreement to Rico's offer. They weren't there to talk about that, and he didn't want to delay the conversation any longer than was necessary. "Normal day for me, you know?"

"So, working at Nocturne," Lucas said with a chuckle. "And people like to accuse me of being a workaholic."

Dan shrugged, giving him a soft smile. "It's become my life, strange as that sounds. And we're an odd sort of family there, I guess."

Lucas nodded and took another deep breath. Dan thought about simply speaking up, making it easier on Lucas, but held himself back. He had always pushed forward, always taken Lucas behind him into something new. It only felt right that if it was to end, if the brakes were going to be slammed down completely, then it should be Lucas who did it.

"I talked to Mateo the other day after the dinner," Lucas began. "And it seems he knows about what's been going on between the two of us."

Dan raised a brow. "Really? I didn't tell him."

"No, it seems one of the employees caught us...in the dressing room. And decided to pass that information along to Mateo."

Dan thought about it for a moment and rolled his eyes. "Glam?"

"Apparently, he *is* quite the gossip."

"That's putting it mildly."

Lucas shook his head. "In any case, it prompted a conversation between my brother and me. I shouldn't be surprised to say that he wasn't bothered in the slightest by what had been happening."

"I can't imagine Mateo would be," Dan mused.

"And it led into...well, it led into him making a few points and asking a question that I wasn't ready for," Lucas told him, looking down at his lap.

"Like what?" Dan asked, both curious and afraid of what was going to be said.

Lucas looked up at the sky again, frowning. "It got me to thinking, turning it over and over in my head. About what we were doing, what it all meant. After spending my whole life one way, I was doing things a different way."

Dan nodded, preparing himself for the speech. He was sure Lucas had it down to the exact word and tone of voice. The man had probably spent most of his free time over the past several days twisting and turning the problem in his head. Thinking it to death, inspecting the body, resurrecting it, only to do it all over again three more times.

"And how we started off calling this friends with benefits, and that was that. How I had the brakes, and you had the gas, and sometimes we shared the steering wheel."

"We did," Dan said quietly, wishing Lucas would simply get it over with. The waiting was almost worse than the blow.

Lucas snorted softly, shaking his head. "And my brother asked me the simplest question, one that made me question everything we've been doing for weeks."

Dan braced himself. "What was that?"

"When I was going to step up and make things serious with you," Lucas said simply

Dan couldn't hold back his surprise. "Mateo asked you that?"

Lucas nodded, turning his attention to Dan and meeting his gaze. "He did. And I realized I had never really asked myself that question before. I'd been so caught up in what was happening, what it could all mean, how I felt about it. I never once looked forward and considered something like that."

"Well," Dan said, trying to give him an easier time of it. "You *are* straight."

Lucas's mouth twisted at the corner in a self-deprecating smile. "Not *that* straight, it seems."

"A little bit of experimenting doesn't change that," Dan said, as much to himself as to Lucas.

Lucas reached out, taking Dan's hand in his and squeezing. "No, it doesn't. But realizing your brother is right, and I should have stopped screwing around weeks ago and treated you like you deserved to be treated, kind of does."

Dan froze, surprise making it hard for him to process what he'd just heard. "Wait, what?"

Lucas cocked his head, an unsure smile on his face. "That is if you're alright with it."

"With what?" Dan demanded, still not comprehending.

"With us. With there being an us in the first place. Stop being friends with benefits, and be...I don't know, boyfriends? Lovers? What's the word people use nowadays?" Lucas asked in sudden confusion.

"Wait...wait," Dan said, shaking his head. "You're *not* here to end things between us?"

Lucas blinked rapidly at him. "No?"

"You're here," Dan began slowly, trying out the words on his tongue. "To ask me to...like, seriously date you? Be in a relationship with me?"

"This is me trying to start a committed relationship with you, so long as you're willing and able," Lucas said, with all the confidence of a lawyer with all the tricks in his bag.

Dan stared and then let out a laugh. "Are you serious?"

Lucas frowned at him. "Of course I'm serious. I would never joke about..."

But Dan had lunged forward, grabbed hold of the man and kissed him fiercely, silencing his indignant protest. Despair and dark anticipation fell away as joy filled Dan's chest, and he gripped onto Lucas tightly as he finished the kiss.

"I thought you were ending things," Dan admitted, panting from the kiss.

"Oh God," Lucas said in horror. "No, God no. I brought you out here so we could talk in private and maybe have a nice sunset to talk under. Just the thought of making you *just* a friend with benefits made me ill and not having you around in my life? I could have been sick from it."

"There's a romantic in there after all," Dan said, tracing the line of Lucas's jaw.

"Perhaps," Lucas said, confidence melting into shyness. "Am I to imagine that this is your way of saying yes?"

"Fuck, yes it is," Dan said with a laugh, wrapping his arms around Lucas's neck and pulling him close.

Lucas laughed with him, burying his face into Dan's neck and holding him tight. Neither of them spoke as they held onto one another, too filled with relief and joy to find words that would work. That was okay by Dan, he had Lucas now, all to himself, and the man wasn't going to go anywhere.

And then he remembered.

Dan jerked back, grinning wide. "Oh! I have the best news."

"Tell me about it," Lucas said gently.

And Dan did.

EPILOGUE

One Year Later

Lucas grunted as he set the heavy box on the bar top. The bottles inside clanked and jingled, but he didn't hear anything break. Opening night was only a few days away, and Dan wanted to make sure everything was ready to go well before the grand opening.

The once dirty building had been absolutely transformed in the course of a year, and Lucas had to give Dan credit. When the man put his mind to something, he threw himself wholeheartedly into it. All the dust, grime, and broken pieces of the building were far in the past.

Standalone archways had been placed along the back wall, atop small platforms. Each platform had a set of stairs that led up to the seating areas at the top. There were collections of stools, ottomans, and couches on each, as well as a table or two for patrons to set their drinks. The center of the place was dominated by a sunken dance floor, rather than the raised one at Nocturne. It was lined by wooden banisters and there was a collection of small tables, big enough for two, around the protective barrier.

Dan had decided to add a balcony up top, extending from one side of the massive room to the other. More seating had been added, as well as a much smaller bar, which was dwarfed by the massive one Dan had installed on the opposite side of the raised seating on the main floor. And everything was decorated in red and gold with warm, almost golden, lights dangling above the seating area, casting just the right amount of shadows to offer privacy when everything was lit up.

"Quit gawking at the scenery," Mateo grumbled as he trudged by Lucas, holding a box of his own and headed toward the back hallway. "There's still more booze."

Lucas rolled his eyes. "Is Dan still giving you shit?"

"I took one little break," Mateo muttered before he disappeared.

Dan's nerves were getting the best of him, and he'd started questioning every little thing he'd decided in the past several months. It had been up to Lucas to help calm the man before, and he was sure that he would have to again. Not that he minded, Dan was easy to pacify, and if he wasn't, there were other ways to get his attention.

Lucas made his way past the bar and into the entryway. He glanced over his head where a sign, composed of golden-colored bulbs and a black background, read *Aria*. It had been another of Dan's ideas, going with the same naming theme as the strip club but doing something a little less risqué sounding.

Christopher was with Dan, who was digging through the moving truck they'd got to move things around between locations. His brother-in-law looked a mixture of amused and anxious as Lucas approached. Without a word, Lucas nodded toward the building, giving Christopher the reprieve he'd been looking for.

"I know it's in here," he heard Dan grumbling, followed by a shuffling noise. "Any luck, Chris?"

"I have relieved him of his solemn charge," Lucas said, watching Dan's ass as it swayed back and forth while the man dug around. "But I've taken over to keep an eye on you."

Dan shot him a dirty look. "You're not helping. You're watching my ass."

"You say that as if that isn't helping *me*."

"Lucas."

He smiled. "What are you looking for?"

"That box of imported liquor," Dan said, eyes roaming the truck's interior hungrily. "I *know* I made sure to grab it from the house."

Lucas sighed, smiled, and held out his hand. "Baby, come here."

If there was one thing Dan was a sucker for, it was being called a cute or sweet name. Any thought of protesting left Dan, and he gave Lucas a wry smile, probably knowing full well what Lucas was doing. But he came, accepting Lucas's hand and hopping out of the truck.

"What?" Dan asked, letting out a huff.

"It was the first thing I took in, just so that the several hundred dollars of expensive alcohol wouldn't risk getting broken," Lucas told him, reaching up to move some of Dan's hair out of his eyes.

Dan let out a sigh of relief. "God, I was afraid we'd left it behind. I just want to get it set up so I don't have to worry about it."

"And we can," Lucas promised him, kissing his brow. "We've got hours. And I've taken the next few days off, so anything you need help with, I'm going to be right there helping."

Dan flashed him a nervous smile. "I just want it to go right."

Lucas's heart went out to the other man. He knew what it was like to want something to go perfectly, even as you knew it could go down in flames. It was exactly how he'd felt just over a year before when he'd finally found the courage to make things official between them. Some part of Lucas's mind had been so sure Dan would turn him away, and yet, he'd accepted him with all the warmth and laughter that Dan was so well known for.

"And it will," Lucas promised him.

"What if it doesn't?"

"Then we'll deal with it. In case you haven't noticed, I'm going to be right here every step of the way."

Dan's anxiety trickled away, and he slumped forward to press his face into Lucas's chest. "Thank you, I know. I've got to be driving everyone crazy by now."

"Mostly yourself," Lucas chuckled.

"Tell me about it," Dan grumbled.

Lucas held him, letting Dan work his anxiety out in his own time. He knew the physical contact would help. Dan was big on physical affection. Whether it was something like a good round of sex or just simply having skin-to-skin contact, it was the way in which Dan showed and received affection the best.

"I love you," Lucas told the other man softly, still warmed every time he said it aloud.

"I love you too," Dan said, looking up fondly.

It had, against all odds, been Lucas who had said it first.

The two of them had been enjoying a picnic at a nearby lake just outside town. Lucas had watched Dan, eyes closed as he turned his face up toward the sun, still wet from the quick dip in the freezing lake, and the words had slipped from his lips before he knew what he was saying. Yet, he'd known he meant it, just as he meant it every time he'd said it since then.

"Hey!" Mateo's outraged voice cut through the moment. "Why the hell am I being put to backbreaking labor while you're out here copping a feel?"

"I *can* put my hands down his pants," Lucas told him, slipping a hand down the back of Dan's pants and squeezing his ass. "Like this."

Dan laughed as Mateo grimaced. Beside him, Christopher was shaking his head, muttering something that sounded suspiciously like, "We deserve this."

"You're a terrible influence on my brother," Mateo accused Dan. "He used to be so innocent."

Dan snorted. "He was not innocent when he met me. Just slow to warm. But don't worry, I warm him up pretty fast."

"Jesus," Mateo groaned, warding Dan off with his hands. "No more! I'm sorry, okay? Just grope him, do whatever, I want no part of this."

Lucas laughed alongside his boyfriend as Mateo went back into the building, with a bemused but chuckling Christopher following close behind. Yeah, maybe Dan had brought out a more wicked side of him, but he wasn't going to argue. In all reality, he and Dan was something Lucas would have never believed could ever happen to him. Not once would he have dreamed that he would find love and a future with another man.

"You're the worst," Lucas told him fondly.

"Yeah, but I'm yours," Dan reminded him with a kiss.

Lucas didn't mind deepening the kiss any more than he minded what Dan had said. Because the other man *was* his, and he had every intention of keeping it that way for as long as they had.